JURASSIC PARK™

VOLUME 4

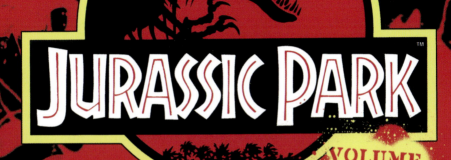

LEAVING JURASSIC PARK

ADAPTED BY
WALTER SIMONSON,
GIL KANE AND GEORGE PEREZ

Spotlight
IDW™

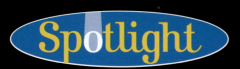

visit us at www.abdopublishing.com

Reinforced library bound editions published in 2014 by Spotlight, a division of the ABDO Group, PO Box 398166, Minneapolis, Minnesota 55439. Published by agreement with IDW Publishing. www.idwpublishing.com

Jurassic Park, and all related character names and distinctive likenesses thereof are trademarks of IDW Publishing and is/are used with permission. Copyright © 2013 IDW Publishing, LLC.

All rights reserved. No portion of this book can be reproduced by any means without permission from IDW Publishing, except for review purposes.

Printed in the United States of America, North Mankato, Minnesota.
052013
092013
♻ This book contains at least 10% recycled materials.

No part of this publication may be reproduced in whole or in part, or stored in a retrieval system, or transmitted in any form or by any means, electronic or mechanical, photocopying, recording, or otherwise without the written permission of the publisher.

Library of Congress Cataloging-in-Publication Data

Simonson, Walter.
 Jurassic Park / adapted by Walter Simonson, Gil Kane, and George Perez.
     pages cm
  ISBN 978-1-61479-183-6 (vol. 1: Danger) -- ISBN 978-1-61479-184-3 (vol. 2: The miracle of cloning) -- ISBN 978-1-61479-185-0 (vol. 3: Don't move!) -- ISBN 978-1-61479-186-7 (vol. 4: Leaving Jurassic Park)
  1. Graphic novels. I. Kane, Gil. II. Perez, George, 1954- III. Title.
 PZ7.7.S5465Jur 2013
 741.5'973--dc23
                           2013011263

All Spotlight books are reinforced library binding and manufactured in the United States of America.

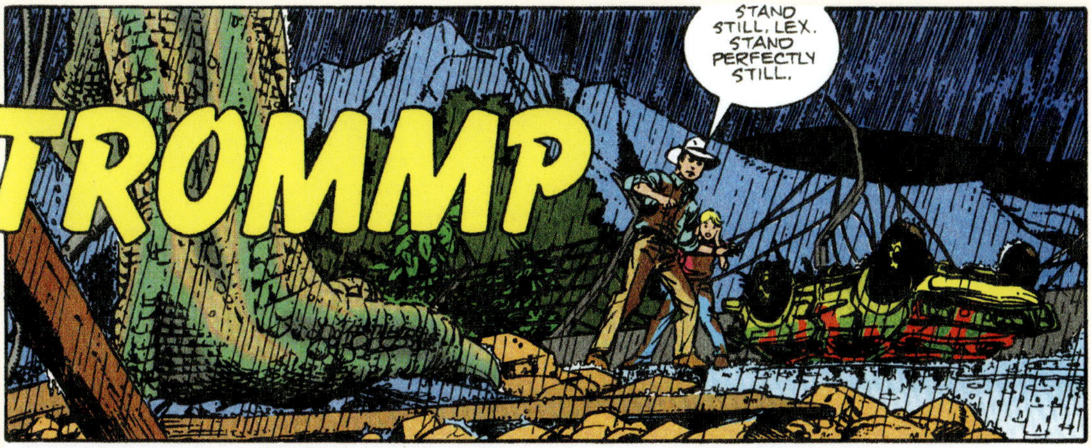
TROMMP
STAND STILL, LEX. STAND PERFECTLY STILL.

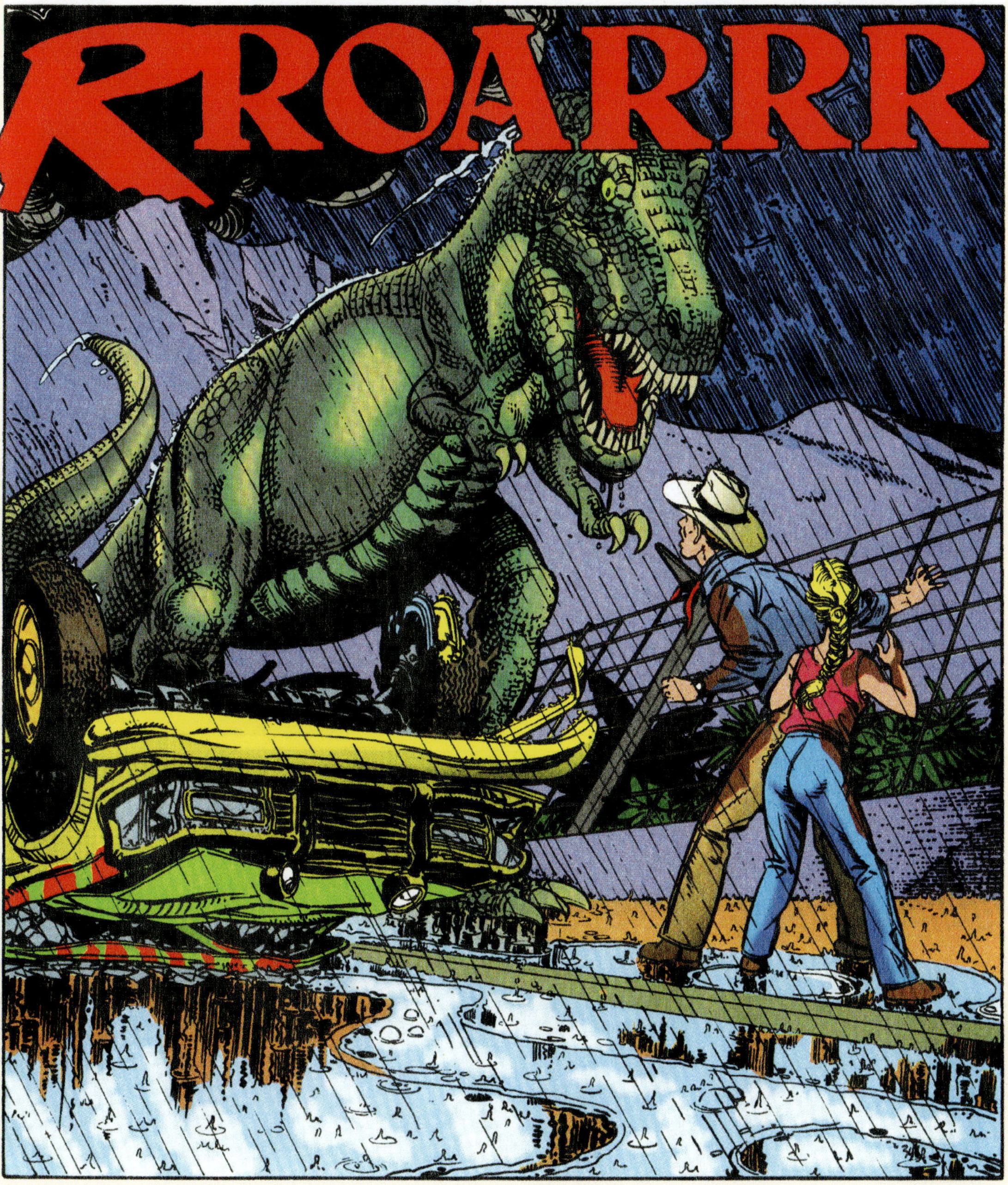
RROARRR

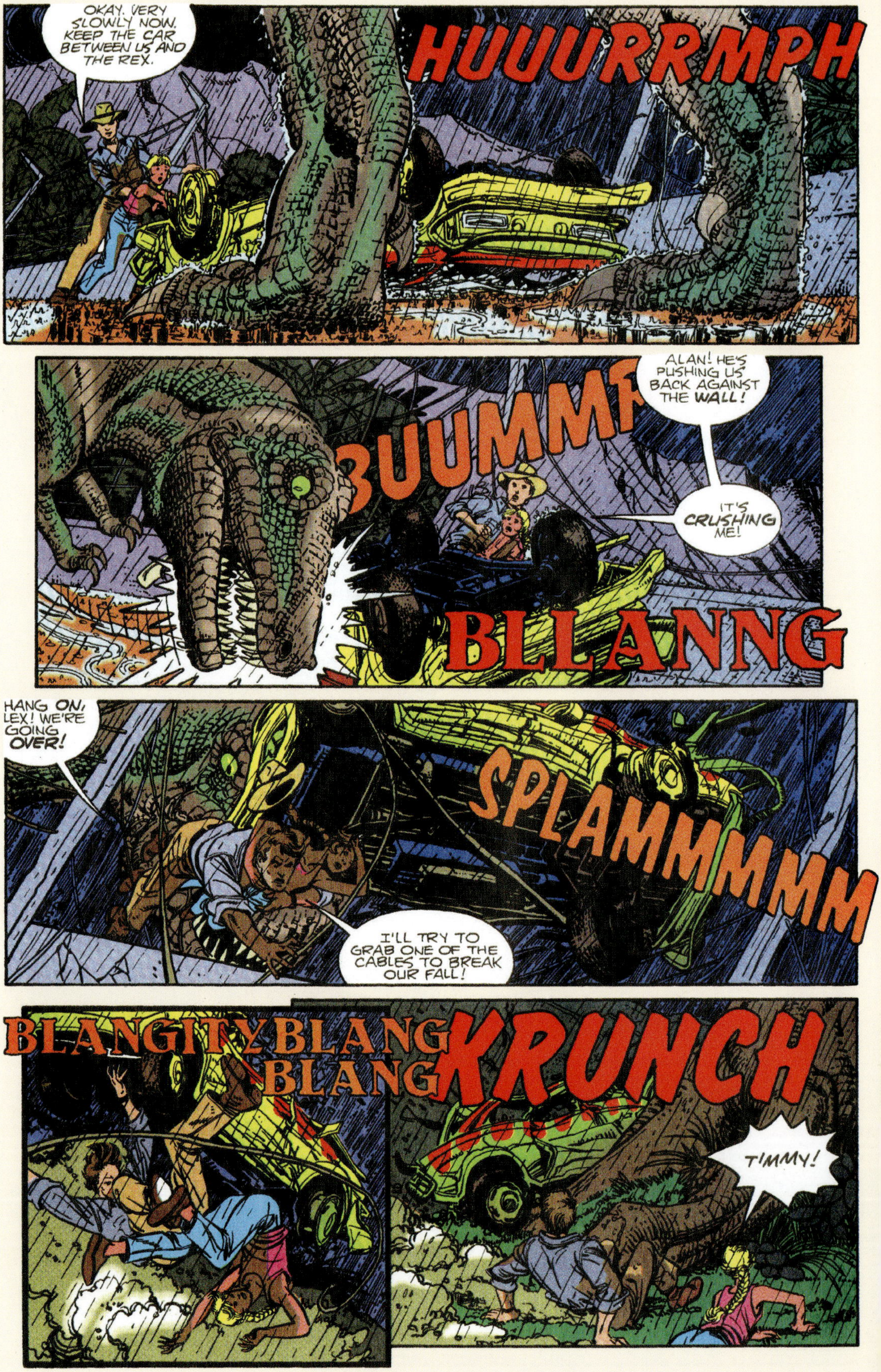
OKAY. VERY SLOWLY NOW. KEEP THE CAR BETWEEN US AND THE REX.
HUUURRMPH
BUUMMF
ALAN! HE'S PUSHING US BACK AGAINST THE WALL!
IT'S CRUSHING ME!
BLLANNG
HANG ON, LEX! WE'RE GOING OVER!
SPLAMMMMMM
I'LL TRY TO GRAB ONE OF THE CABLES TO BREAK OUR FALL!
BLANGITY BLANG BLANG BLANG
KRUNCH
TIMMY!

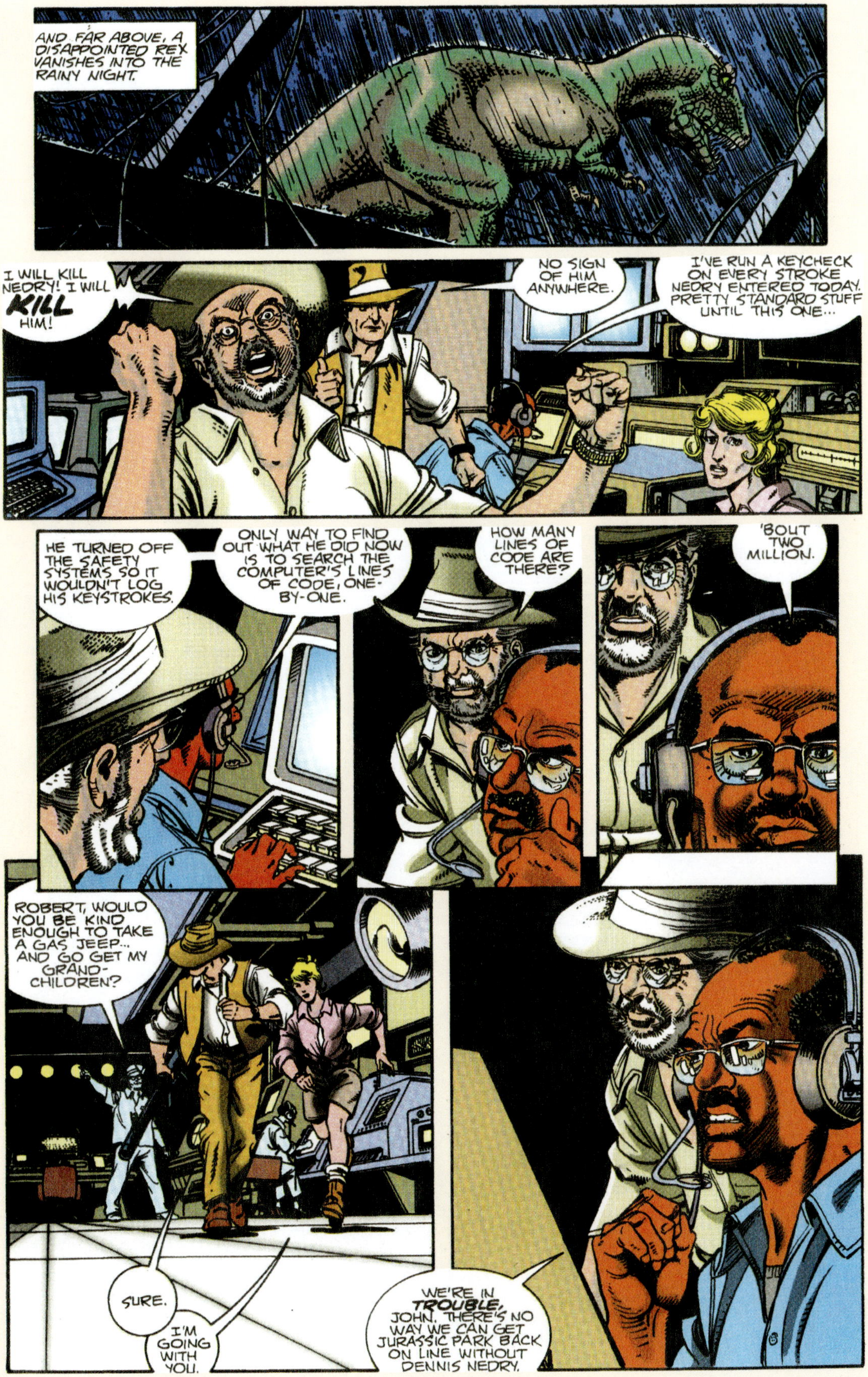
AND FAR ABOVE, A DISAPPOINTED REX VANISHES INTO THE RAINY NIGHT.
I WILL KILL NEDRY! I WILL KILL HIM!
NO SIGN OF HIM ANYWHERE.
I'VE RUN A KEYCHECK ON EVERY STROKE NEDRY ENTERED TODAY. PRETTY STANDARD STUFF UNTIL THIS ONE...
HE TURNED OFF THE SAFETY SYSTEMS SO IT WOULDN'T LOG HIS KEYSTROKES.
ONLY WAY TO FIND OUT WHAT HE DID NOW IS TO SEARCH THE COMPUTER'S LINES OF CODE, ONE-BY-ONE.
HOW MANY LINES OF CODE ARE THERE?
'BOUT TWO MILLION.
ROBERT, WOULD YOU BE KIND ENOUGH TO TAKE A GAS JEEP... AND GO GET MY GRAND-CHILDREN?
SURE.
I'M GOING WITH YOU.
WE'RE IN TROUBLE, JOHN. THERE'S NO WAY WE CAN GET JURASSIC PARK BACK ON LINE WITHOUT DENNIS NEDRY.

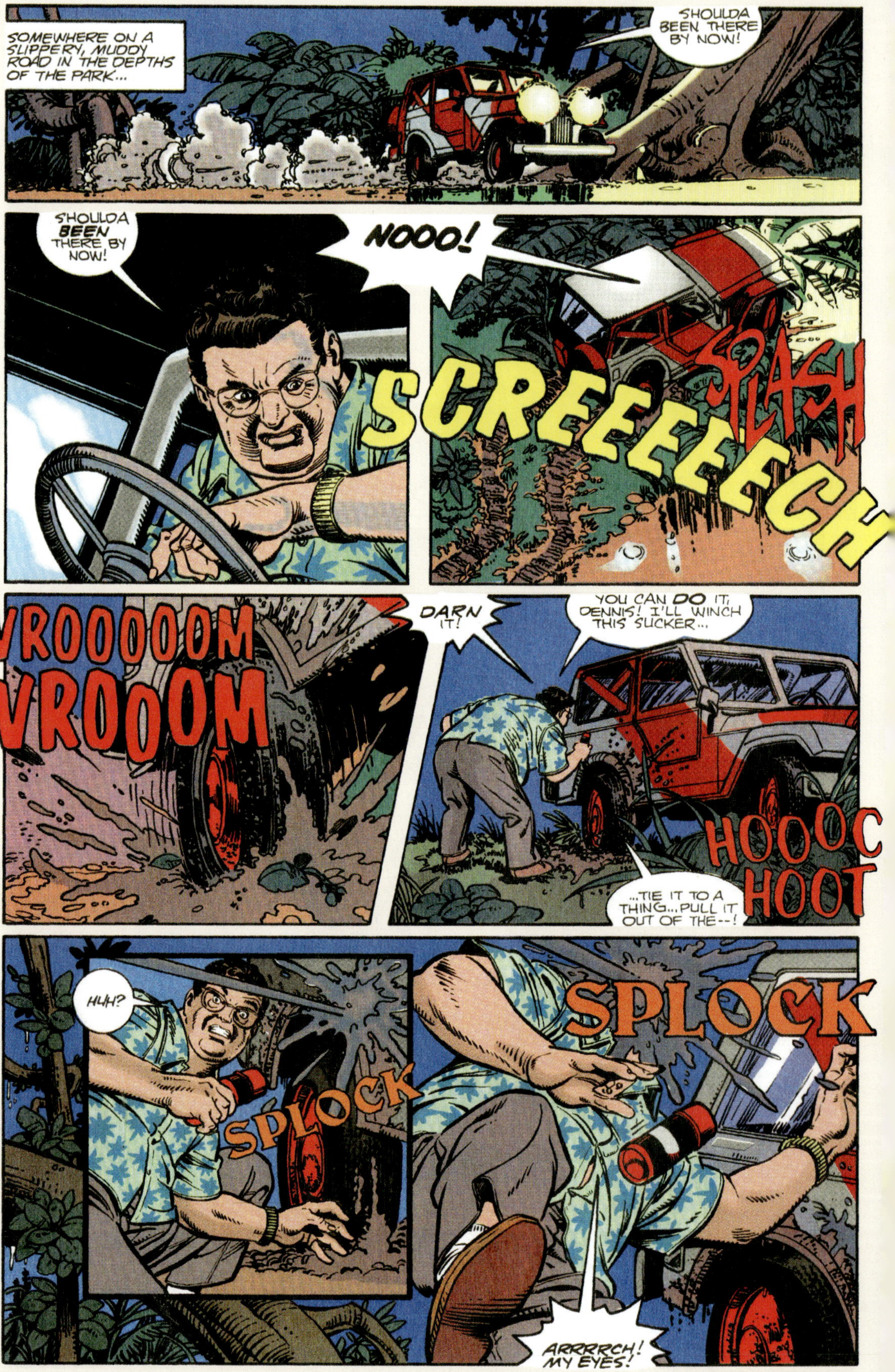
SOMEWHERE ON A SLIPPERY, MUDDY ROAD IN THE DEPTHS OF THE PARK...
SHOULDA BEEN THERE BY NOW!
SHOULDA BEEN THERE BY NOW!
NOOO!
SCREEEEECH
SPLASH
VROOOOOM
VROOOM
DARN IT!
YOU CAN DO IT, DENNIS! I'LL WINCH THIS SUCKER...
...TIE IT TO A THING...PULL IT OUT OF THE--!
HOOOC
HOOT
HUH?
SPLOCK
SPLOCK
ARRRRCH! MY EYES!

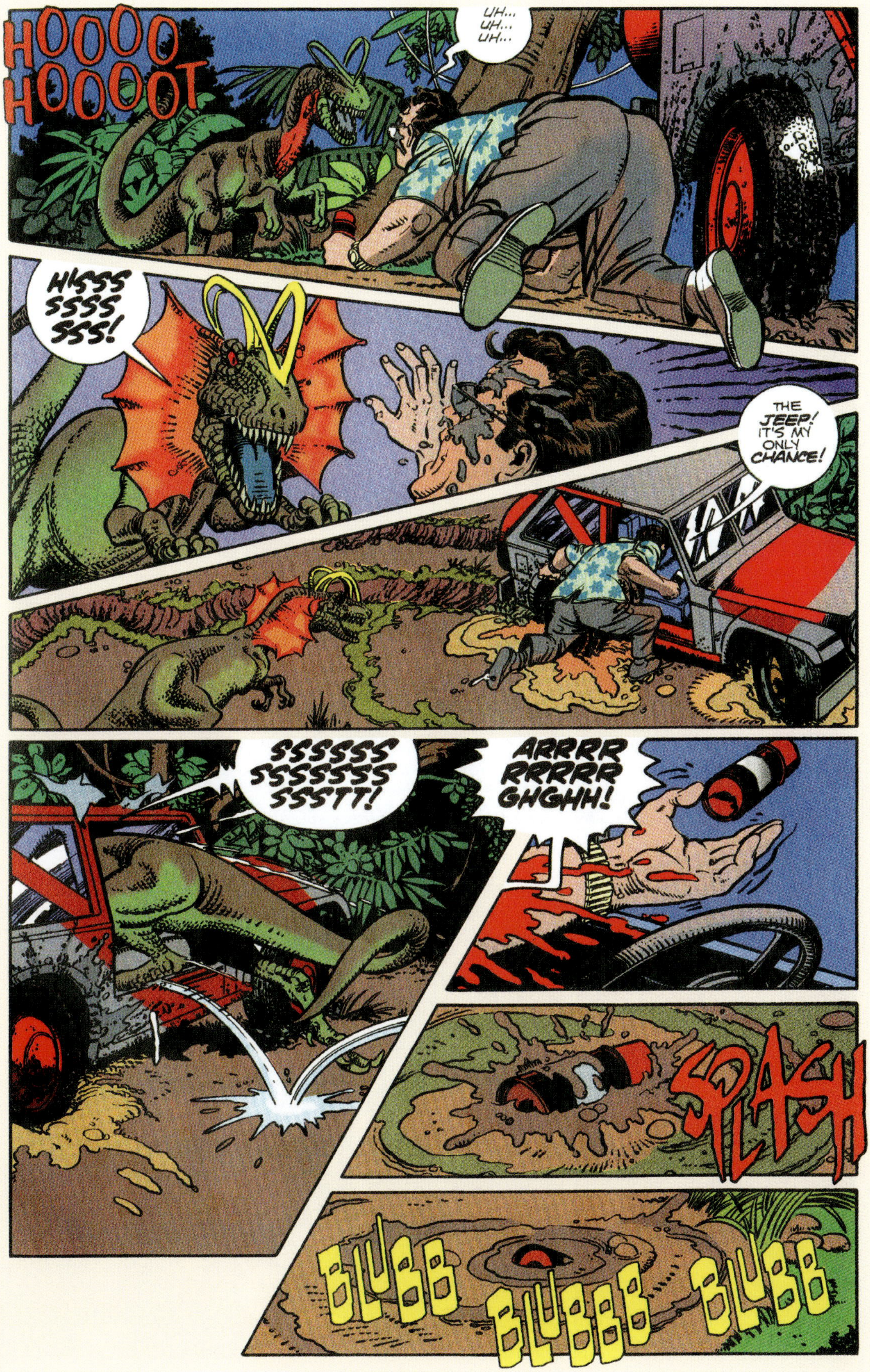
HOOOO HOOOOT
UH... UH... UH...
HISSS SSSS SSS!
THE JEEP! IT'S MY ONLY CHANCE!
SSSSSS SSSSSSS SSSTT!
ARRRR RRRRR GHGHH!
SPLASH
BLUBB BLUBBB BLUBB

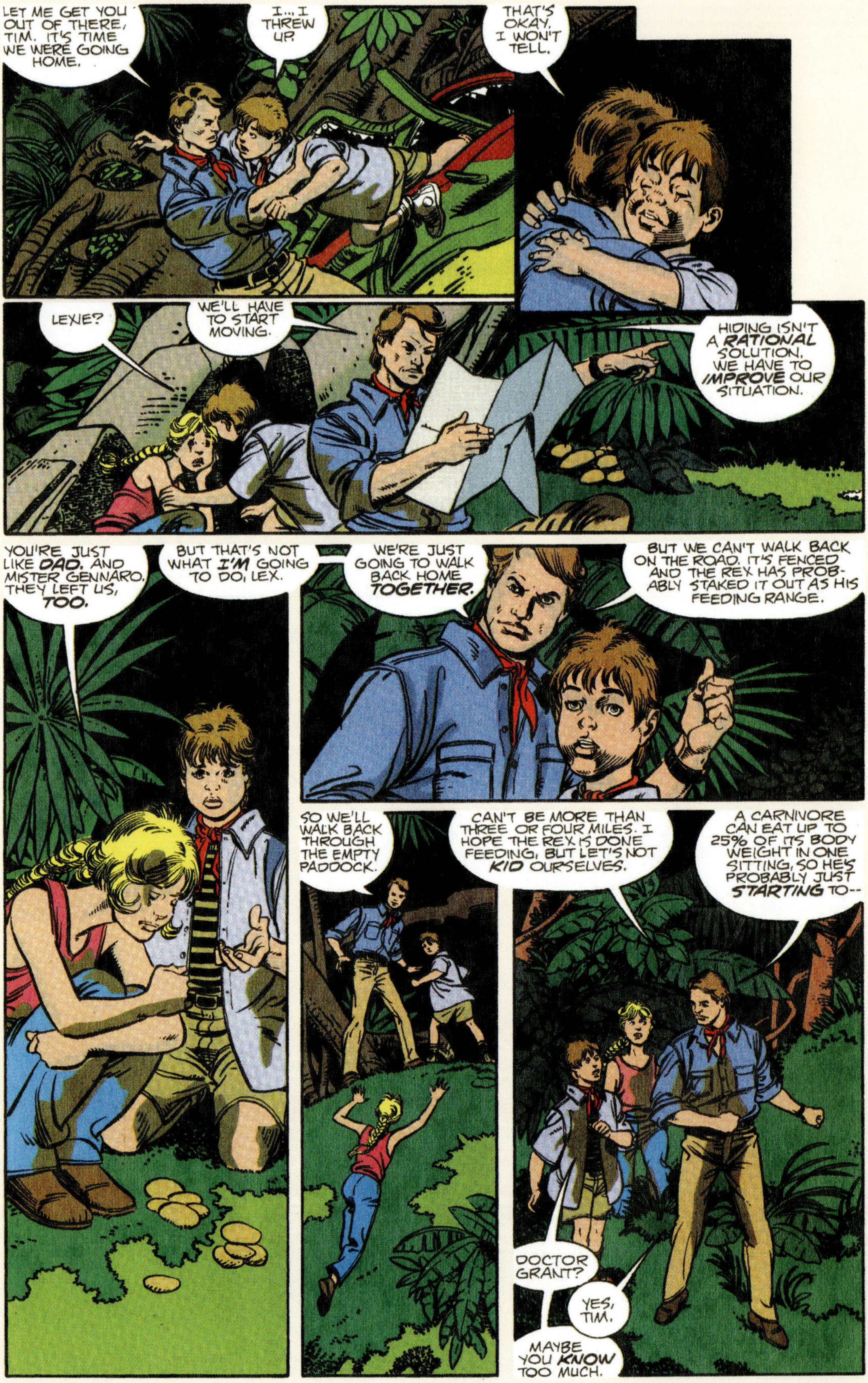
LET ME GET YOU OUT OF THERE, TIM. IT'S TIME WE WERE GOING HOME.
I... I THREW UP.
THAT'S OKAY. I WON'T TELL.
LEXIE?
WE'LL HAVE TO START MOVING.
HIDING ISN'T A **RATIONAL** SOLUTION. WE HAVE TO **IMPROVE** OUR SITUATION.
YOU'RE JUST LIKE **DAD.** AND MISTER GENNARO. THEY LEFT US, **TOO.**
BUT THAT'S NOT WHAT **I'M** GOING TO DO, LEX.
WE'RE JUST GOING TO WALK BACK HOME **TOGETHER.**
BUT WE CAN'T WALK BACK ON THE ROAD. IT'S FENCED AND THE REX HAS PROBABLY STAKED IT OUT AS HIS FEEDING RANGE.
SO WE'LL WALK BACK THROUGH THE EMPTY PADDOCK.
CAN'T BE MORE THAN THREE OR FOUR MILES. I HOPE THE REX IS DONE FEEDING, BUT LET'S NOT **KID** OURSELVES.
A CARNIVORE CAN EAT UP TO 25% OF ITS BODY WEIGHT IN ONE SITTING, SO HE'S PROBABLY JUST **STARTING** TO--
DOCTOR GRANT?
YES, TIM.
MAYBE YOU **KNOW** TOO MUCH.

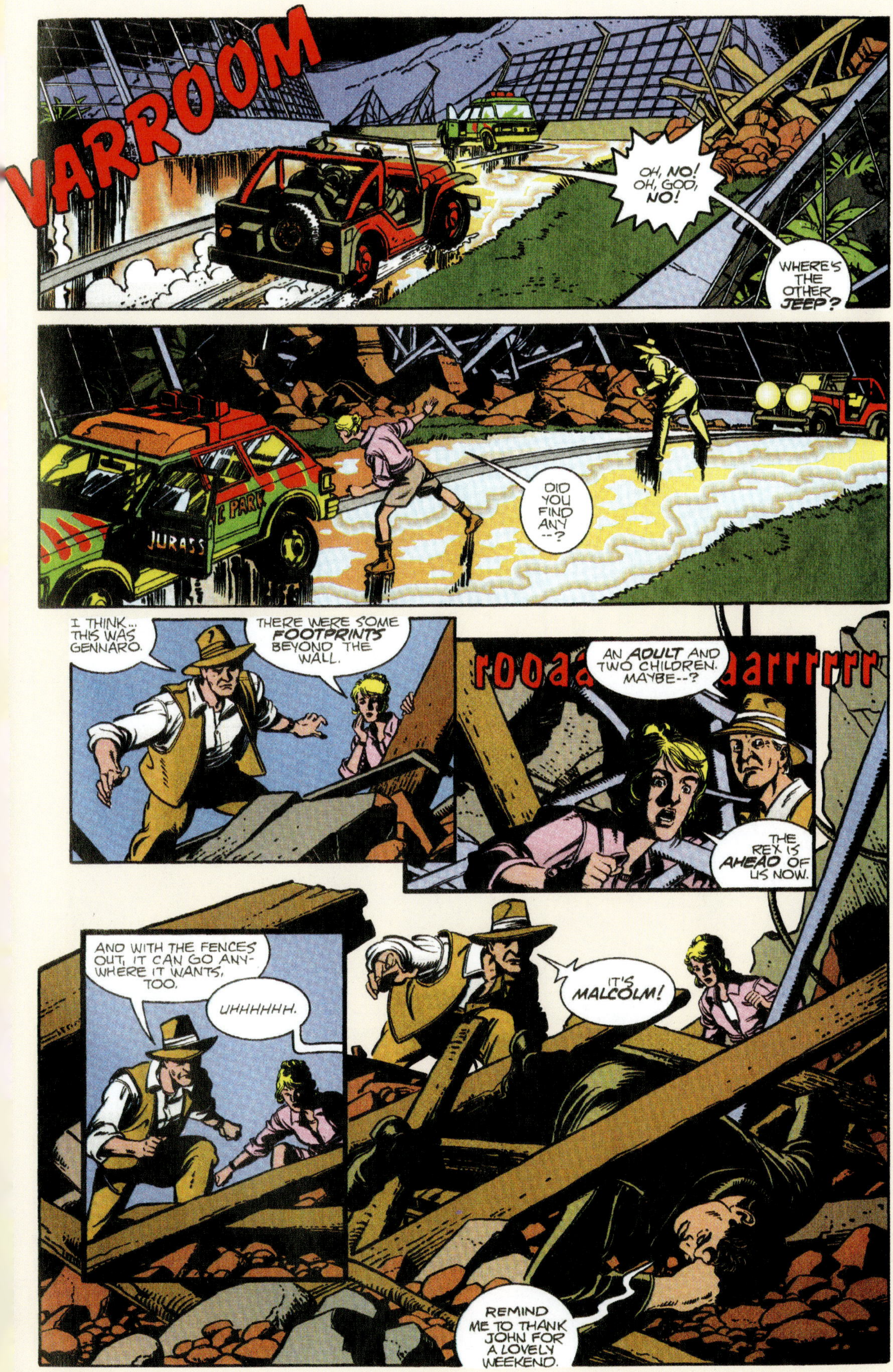
VARROOM
OH, NO! OH, GOD, NO!
WHERE'S THE OTHER JEEP?
DID YOU FIND ANY --?
I THINK... THIS WAS GENNARO.
THERE WERE SOME FOOTPRINTS BEYOND THE WALL.
AN ADULT AND TWO CHILDREN. MAYBE--?
rooaa aarrrrrr
THE REX IS AHEAD OF US NOW.
AND WITH THE FENCES OUT, IT CAN GO ANY-WHERE IT WANTS, TOO.
UHHHHHH.
IT'S MALCOLM!
REMIND ME TO THANK JOHN FOR A LOVELY WEEKEND.

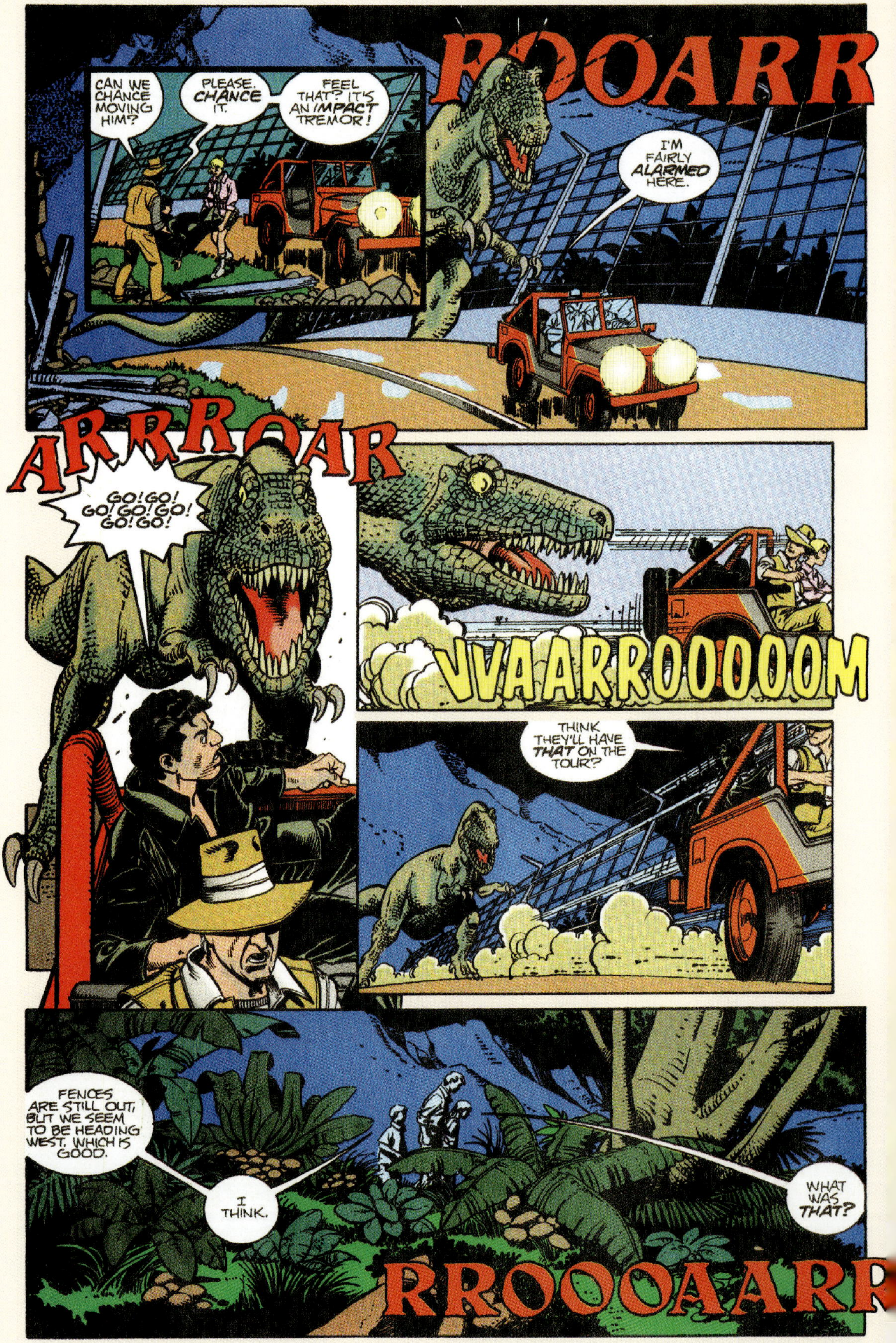

ROOARR
CAN WE CHANCE MOVING HIM?
PLEASE. CHANCE IT.
FEEL THAT? IT'S AN IMPACT TREMOR!
I'M FAIRLY ALARMED HERE.
ARRROAR
GO! GO! GO! GO! GO! GO! GO!
VVAARROOOOOM
THINK THEY'LL HAVE THAT ON THE TOUR?
FENCES ARE STILL OUT, BUT WE SEEM TO BE HEADING WEST. WHICH IS GOOD.
I THINK.
WHAT WAS THAT?
RROOOAARR

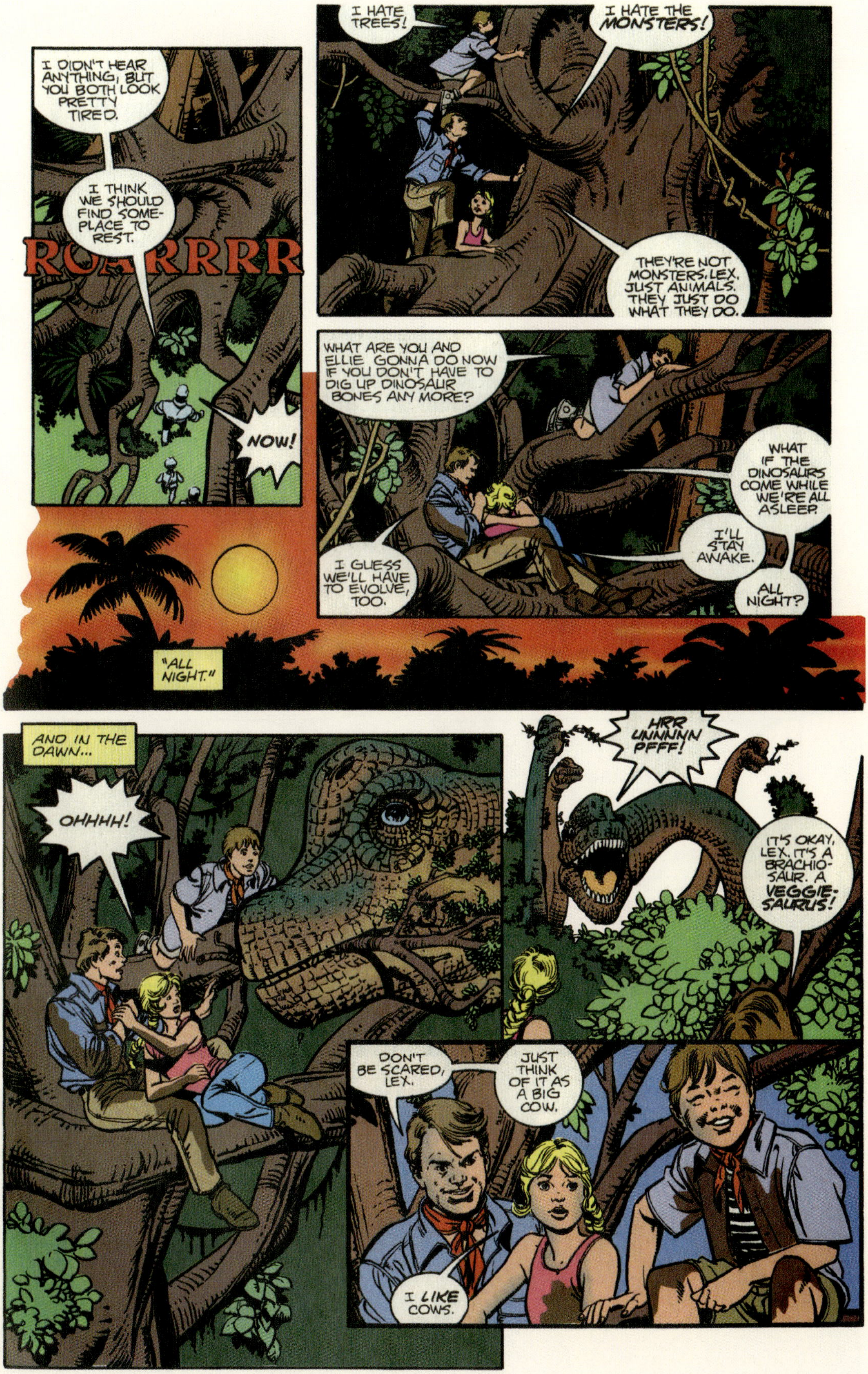
I DIDN'T HEAR ANYTHING, BUT YOU BOTH LOOK PRETTY TIRED.
I THINK WE SHOULD FIND SOME-PLACE TO REST.
ROARRRRR
NOW!
I HATE TREES!
I HATE THE MONSTERS!
THEY'RE NOT MONSTERS, LEX. JUST ANIMALS. THEY JUST DO WHAT THEY DO.
WHAT ARE YOU AND ELLIE GONNA DO NOW IF YOU DON'T HAVE TO DIG UP DINOSAUR BONES ANY MORE?
I GUESS WE'LL HAVE TO EVOLVE, TOO.
WHAT IF THE DINOSAURS COME WHILE WE'RE ALL ASLEEP?
I'LL STAY AWAKE.
ALL NIGHT?
"ALL NIGHT."
AND IN THE DAWN...
OHHHH!
HRR UNNNNN PFFF!
IT'S OKAY, LEX. IT'S A BRACHIO-SAUR. A VEGGIE-SAURUS!
DON'T BE SCARED, LEX.
JUST THINK OF IT AS A BIG COW.
I LIKE COWS.

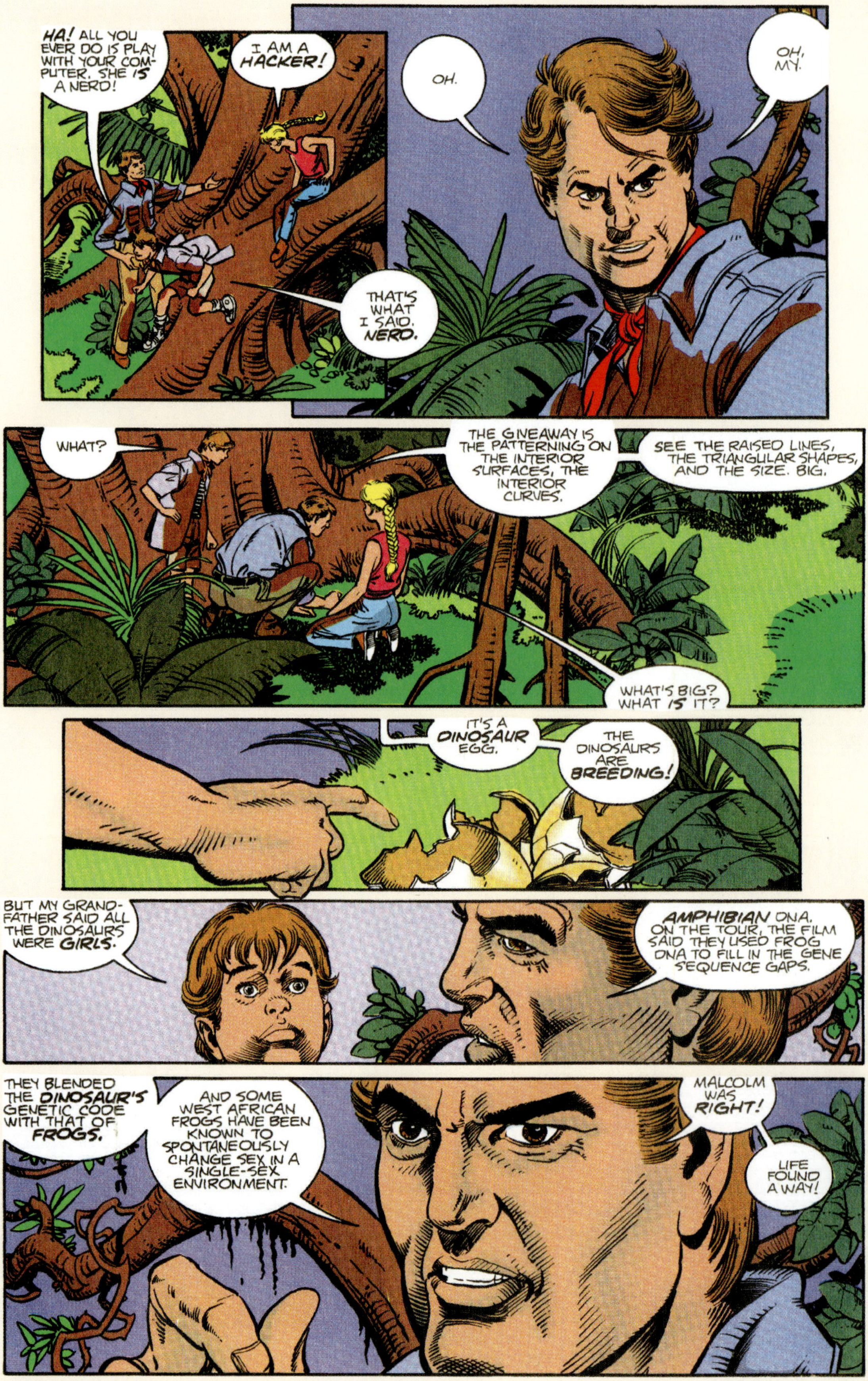
HA! ALL YOU EVER DO IS PLAY WITH YOUR COMPUTER. SHE IS A NERD!
I AM A HACKER!
THAT'S WHAT I SAID. NERD.
OH.
OH, MY.
WHAT?
THE GIVEAWAY IS THE PATTERNING ON THE INTERIOR SURFACES, THE INTERIOR CURVES.
SEE THE RAISED LINES, THE TRIANGULAR SHAPES, AND THE SIZE. BIG.
WHAT'S BIG? WHAT IS IT?
IT'S A DINOSAUR EGG.
THE DINOSAURS ARE BREEDING!
BUT MY GRANDFATHER SAID ALL THE DINOSAURS WERE GIRLS.
AMPHIBIAN DNA. ON THE TOUR, THE FILM SAID THEY USED FROG DNA TO FILL IN THE GENE SEQUENCE GAPS.
THEY BLENDED THE DINOSAUR'S GENETIC CODE WITH THAT OF FROGS.
AND SOME WEST AFRICAN FROGS HAVE BEEN KNOWN TO SPONTANEOUSLY CHANGE SEX IN A SINGLE-SEX ENVIRONMENT.
MALCOLM WAS RIGHT!
LIFE FOUND A WAY!

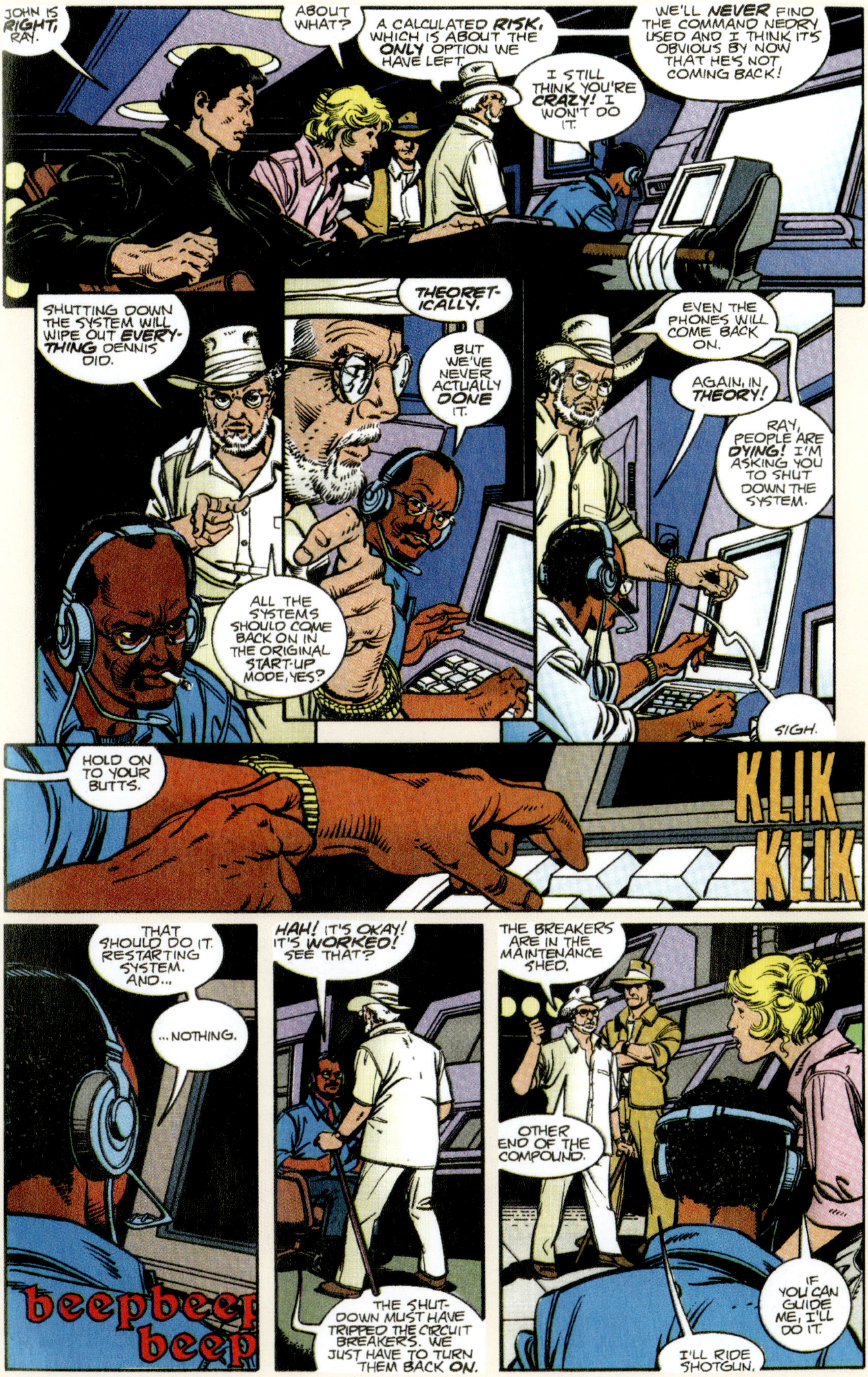
JOHN IS RIGHT, RAY.
ABOUT WHAT?
A CALCULATED RISK, WHICH IS ABOUT THE ONLY OPTION WE HAVE LEFT.
I STILL THINK YOU'RE CRAZY! I WON'T DO IT.
WE'LL NEVER FIND THE COMMAND NEDRY USED AND I THINK IT'S OBVIOUS BY NOW THAT HE'S NOT COMING BACK!
SHUTTING DOWN THE SYSTEM WILL WIPE OUT EVERYTHING DENNIS DID.
ALL THE SYSTEMS SHOULD COME BACK ON IN THE ORIGINAL START-UP MODE, YES?
THEORETICALLY.
BUT WE'VE NEVER ACTUALLY DONE IT.
EVEN THE PHONES WILL COME BACK ON.
AGAIN, IN THEORY!
RAY, PEOPLE ARE DYING! I'M ASKING YOU TO SHUT DOWN THE SYSTEM.
SIGH.
HOLD ON TO YOUR BUTTS.
KLIK KLIK
THAT SHOULD DO IT. RESTARTING SYSTEM. AND...
...NOTHING.
beepbeep beep
HAH! IT'S OKAY! IT'S WORKED! SEE THAT?
THE SHUT-DOWN MUST HAVE TRIPPED THE CIRCUIT BREAKERS. WE JUST HAVE TO TURN THEM BACK ON.
THE BREAKERS ARE IN THE MAINTENANCE SHED.
OTHER END OF THE COMPOUND.
IF YOU CAN GUIDE ME, I'LL DO IT.
I'LL RIDE SHOTGUN.

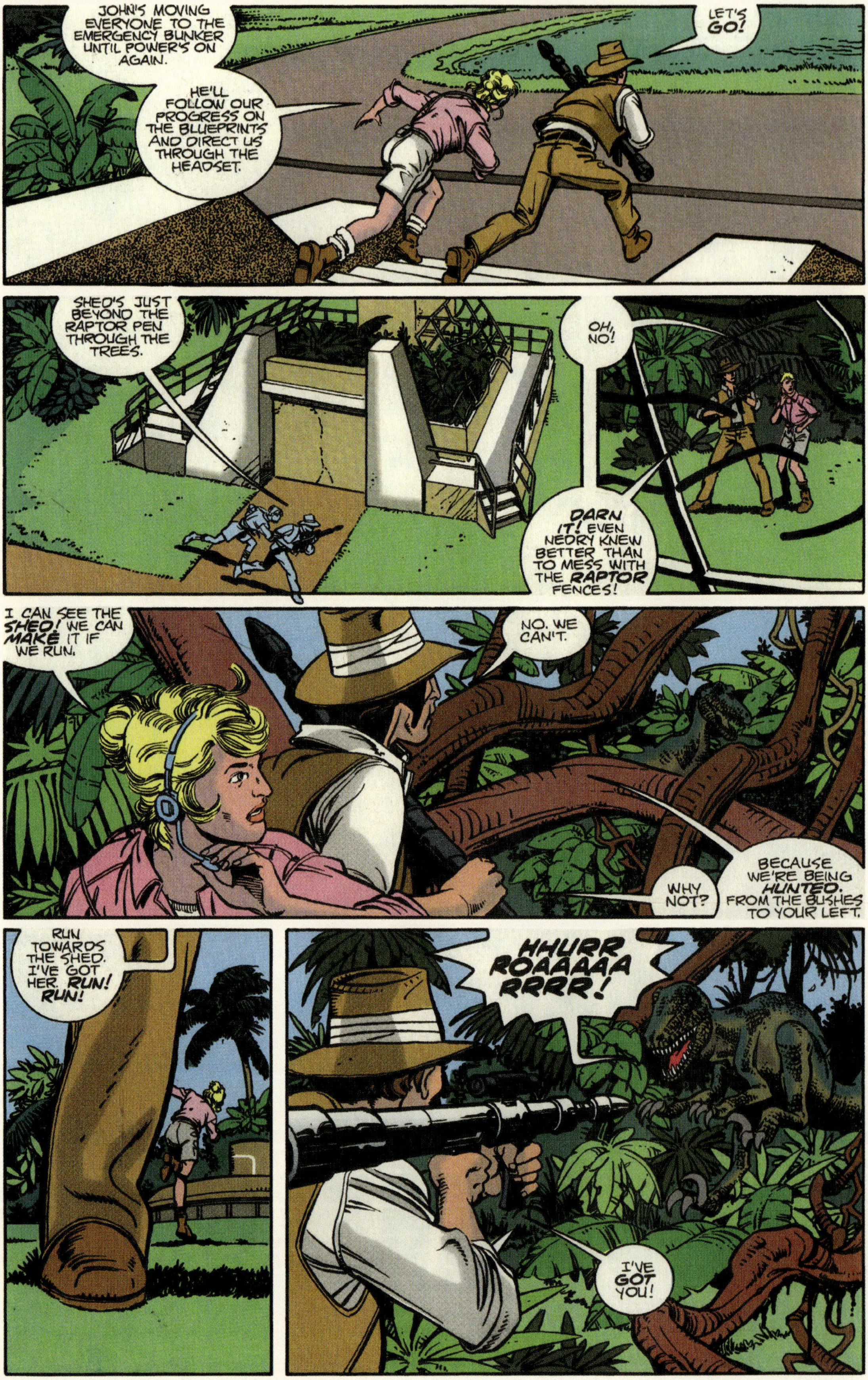
JOHN'S MOVING EVERYONE TO THE EMERGENCY BUNKER UNTIL POWER'S ON AGAIN.
HE'LL FOLLOW OUR PROGRESS ON THE BLUEPRINTS AND DIRECT US THROUGH THE HEADSET.
LET'S GO!
SHED'S JUST BEYOND THE RAPTOR PEN THROUGH THE TREES.
OH, NO!
DARN IT! EVEN NEDRY KNEW BETTER THAN TO MESS WITH THE RAPTOR FENCES!
I CAN SEE THE SHED! WE CAN MAKE IT IF WE RUN.
NO. WE CAN'T.
WHY NOT?
BECAUSE WE'RE BEING HUNTED. FROM THE BUSHES TO YOUR LEFT.
RUN TOWARDS THE SHED. I'VE GOT HER. RUN! RUN!
HHURR ROAAAAA RRRR!
I'VE GOT YOU!

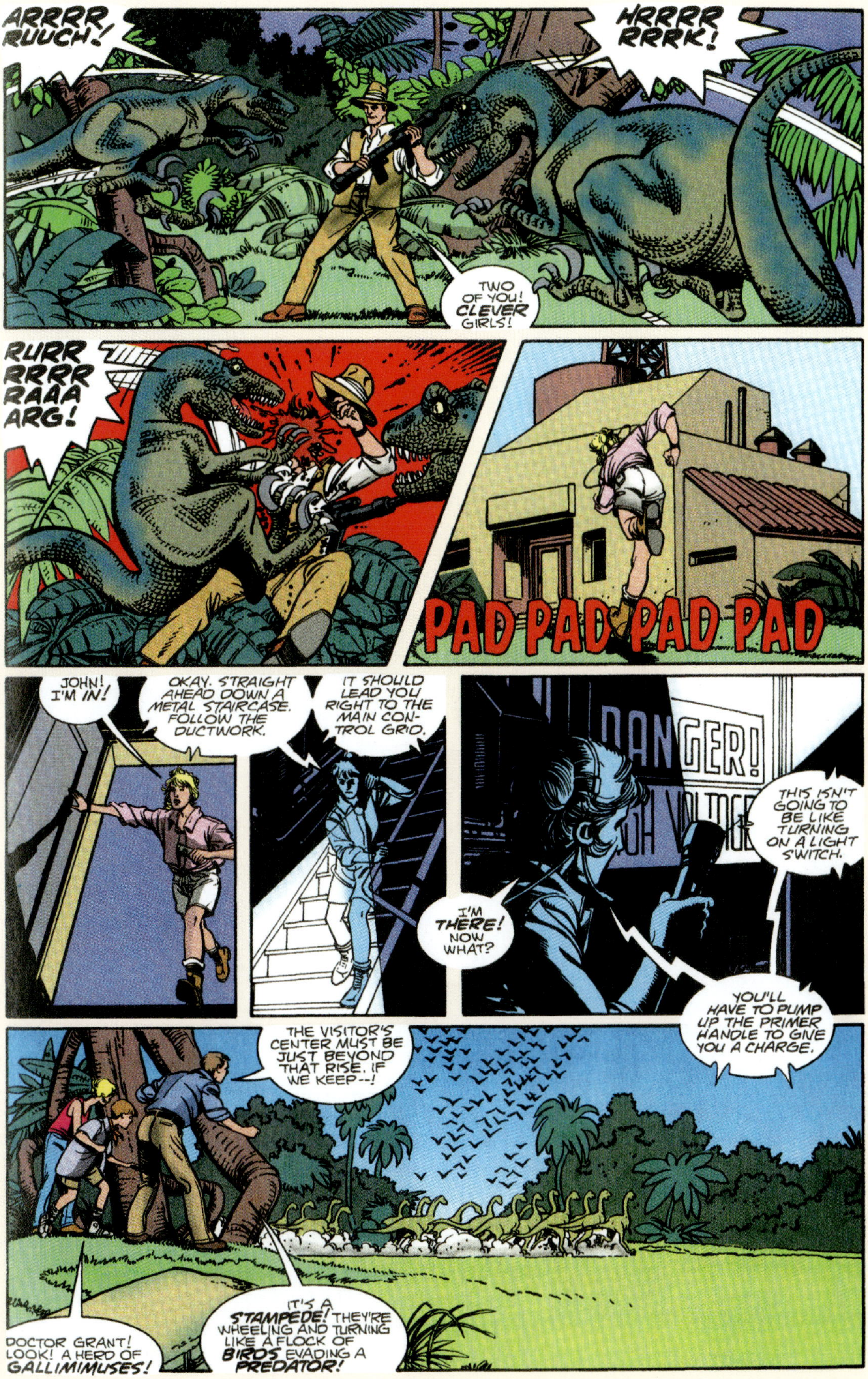
ARRRR RUUCH!
HRRRR RRRK!
TWO OF YOU! CLEVER GIRLS!
RURR RRRR RAAA ARG!
PAD PAD PAD PAD
JOHN! I'M IN!
OKAY. STRAIGHT AHEAD DOWN A METAL STAIRCASE. FOLLOW THE DUCTWORK.
IT SHOULD LEAD YOU RIGHT TO THE MAIN CONTROL GRID.
DANGER!
THIS ISN'T GOING TO BE LIKE TURNING ON A LIGHT SWITCH.
I'M THERE! NOW WHAT?
YOU'LL HAVE TO PUMP UP THE PRIMER HANDLE TO GIVE YOU A CHARGE.
THE VISITOR'S CENTER MUST BE JUST BEYOND THAT RISE. IF WE KEEP--!
DOCTOR GRANT! LOOK! A HERD OF GALLIMIMUSES!
IT'S A STAMPEDE! THEY'RE WHEELING AND TURNING LIKE A FLOCK OF BIRDS EVADING A PREDATOR!

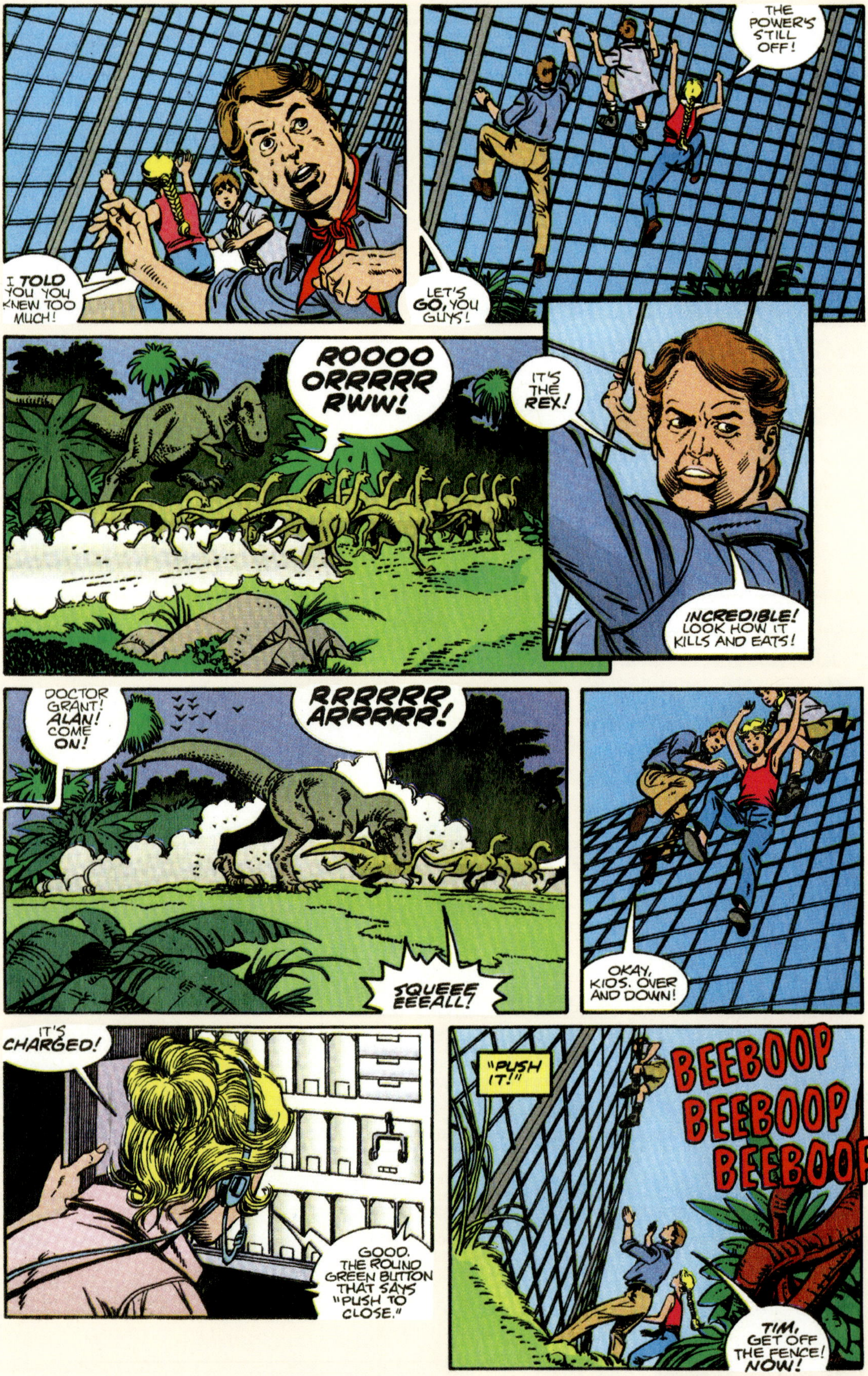
I TOLD YOU YOU KNEW TOO MUCH!
LET'S GO, YOU GUYS!
THE POWER'S STILL OFF!
ROOOO ORRRRR RWW!
IT'S THE REX!
INCREDIBLE! LOOK HOW IT KILLS AND EATS!
DOCTOR GRANT! ALAN! COME ON!
RRRRRR ARRRRR!
SQUEEE EEEALL!
OKAY, KIDS. OVER AND DOWN!
IT'S CHARGED!
GOOD. THE ROUND GREEN BUTTON THAT SAYS "PUSH TO CLOSE."
"PUSH IT!"
BEEBOOP BEEBOOP BEEBOOP
TIM, GET OFF THE FENCE! NOW!

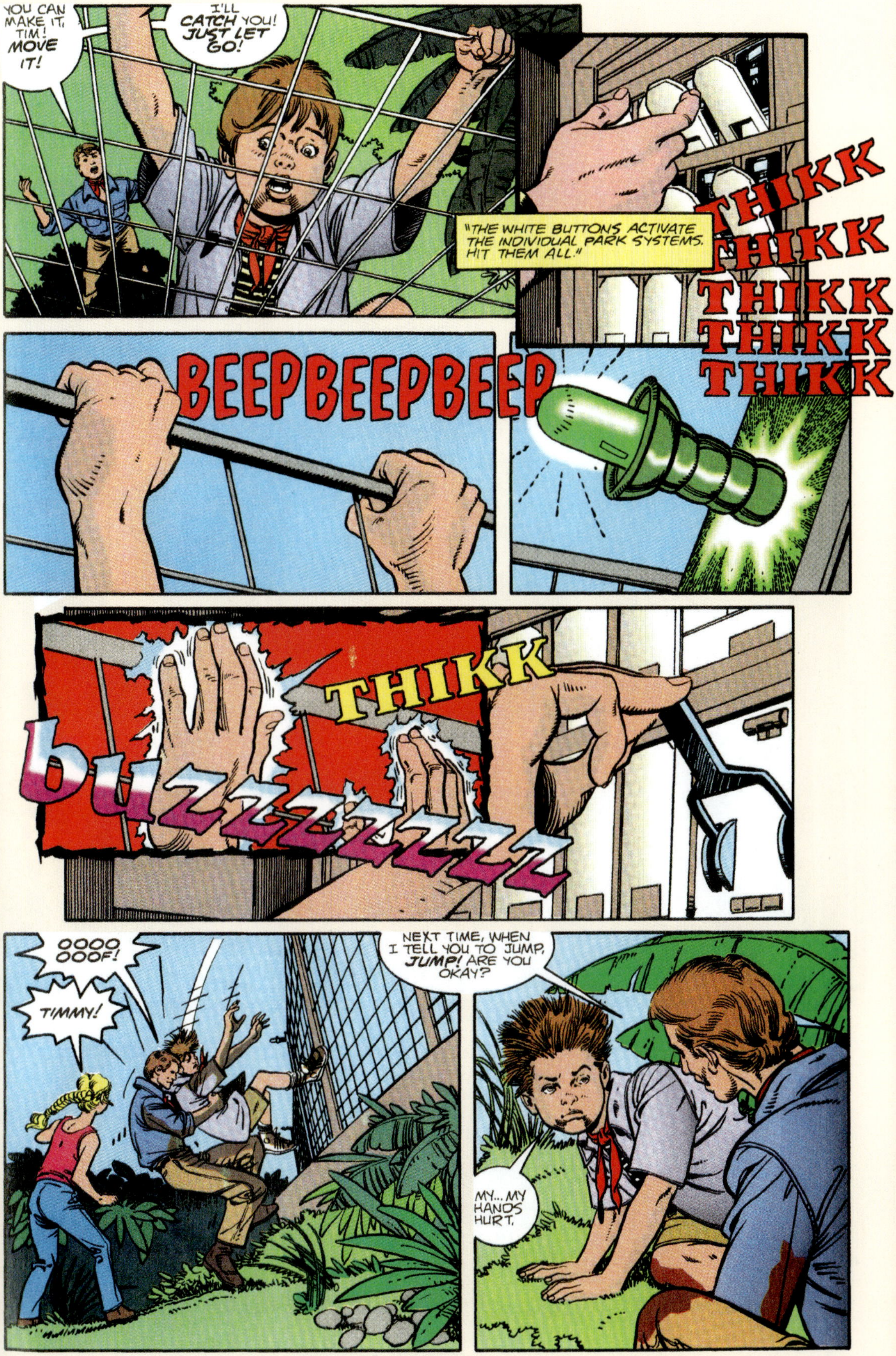
YOU CAN MAKE IT, TIM! MOVE IT!
I'LL CATCH YOU! JUST LET GO!
"THE WHITE BUTTONS ACTIVATE THE INDIVIDUAL PARK SYSTEMS. HIT THEM ALL."
THIKK THIKK THIKK THIKK THIKK
BEEPBEEPBEEP
THIKK
buzzzzzzzz
OOOO OOOF!
TIMMY!
NEXT TIME, WHEN I TELL YOU TO JUMP, JUMP! ARE YOU OKAY?
MY... MY HANDS HURT.

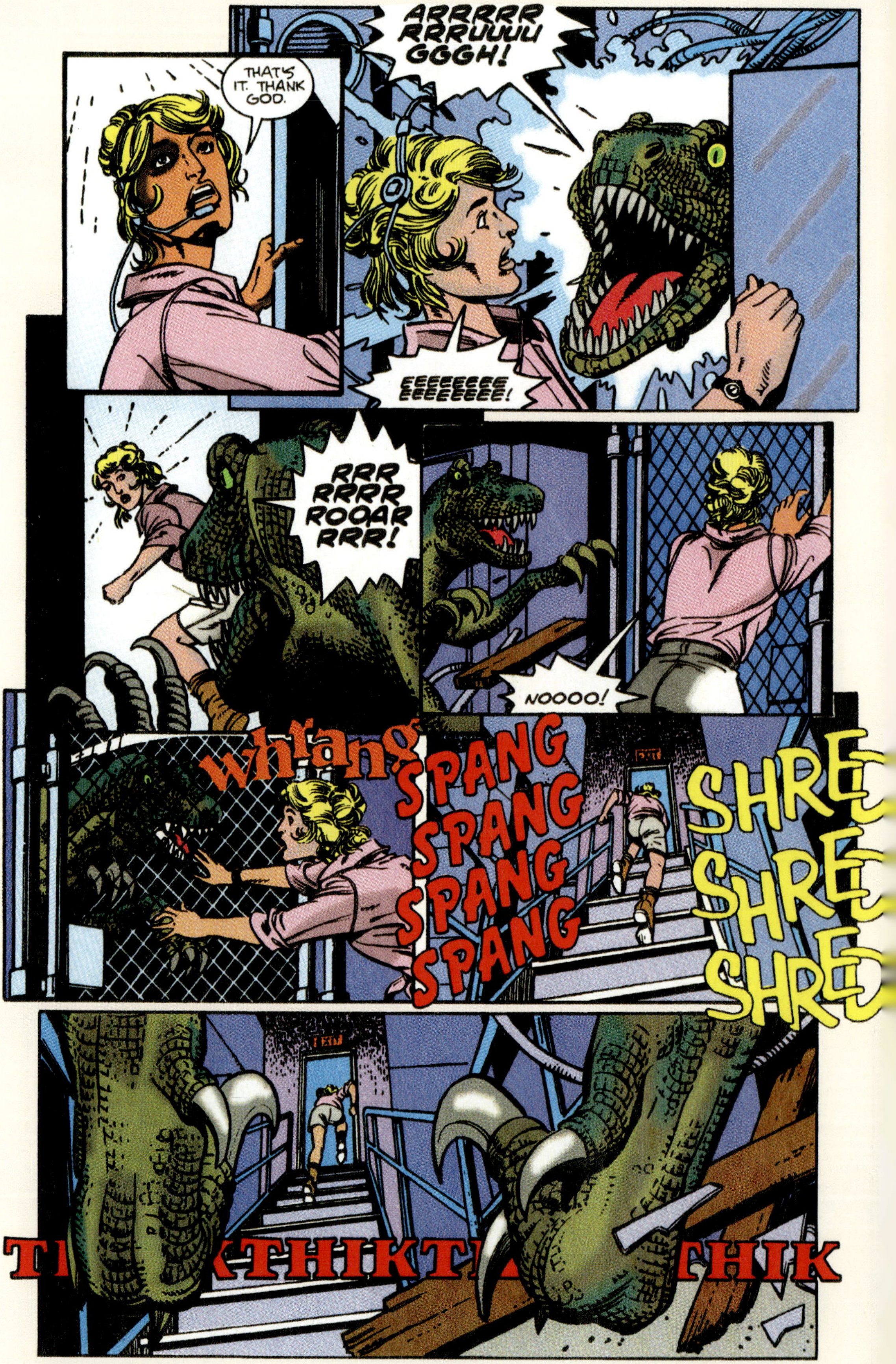
THAT'S IT. THANK GOD.
ARRRRRR RRRUUUU GGGH!
EEEEEEEE EEEEEEEEE!
RRR RRRR ROOAR RRR!
NOOOO!
whrang
SPANG SPANG SPANG SPANG
EXIT
SHRED SHRED SHRED
EXIT
THIK

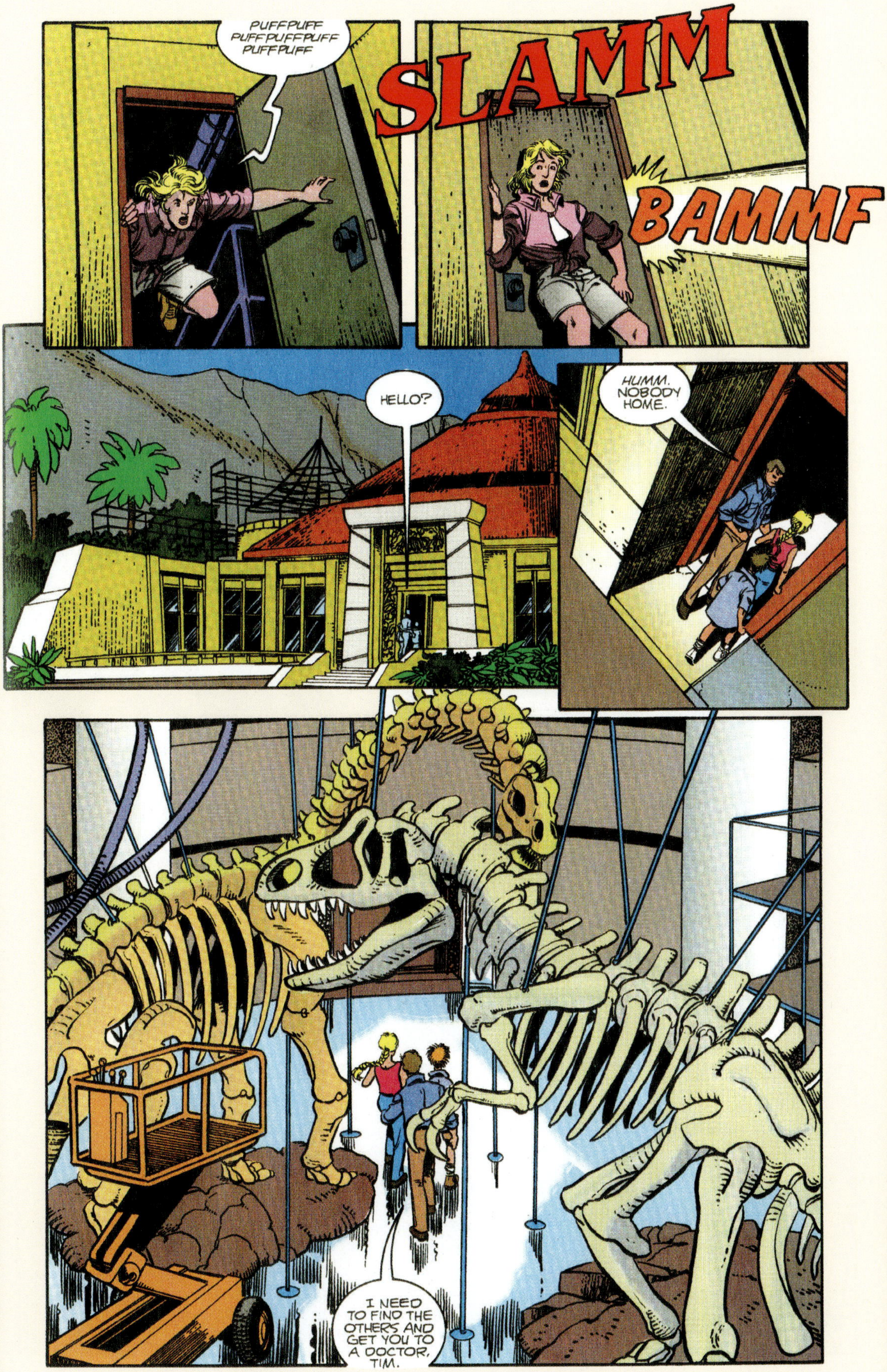
PUFFPUFF PUFFPUFFPUFF PUFFPUFF
SLAMM
BAMMF
HELLO?
HUMM. NOBODY HOME.
I NEED TO FIND THE OTHERS AND GET YOU TO A DOCTOR, TIM.

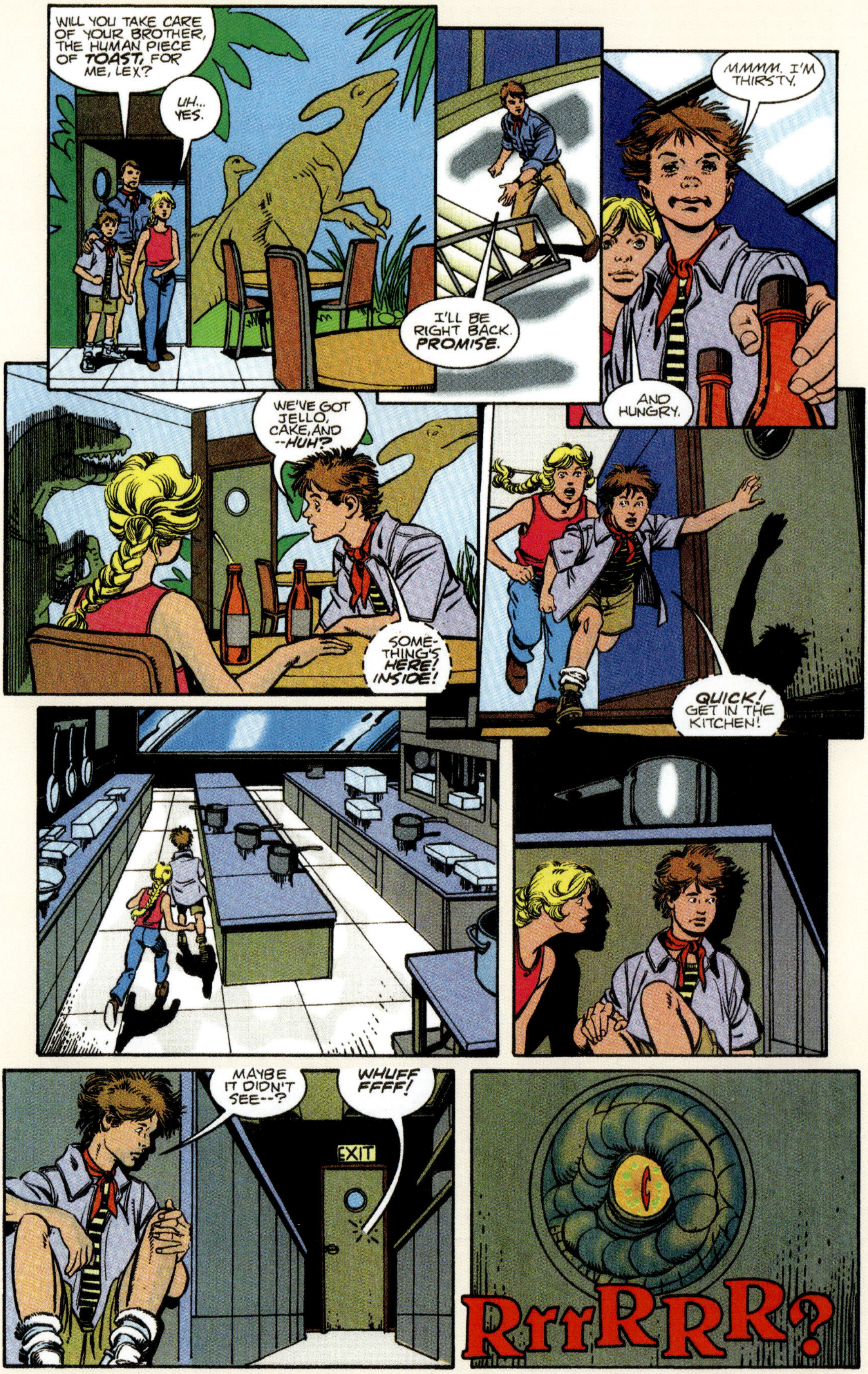
WILL YOU TAKE CARE OF YOUR BROTHER, THE HUMAN PIECE OF TOAST, FOR ME, LEX?
UH... YES.
I'LL BE RIGHT BACK. PROMISE.
MMMM. I'M THIRSTY.
AND HUNGRY.
WE'VE GOT JELLO, CAKE, AND --HUH?
SOME-THING'S HERE! INSIDE!
QUICK! GET IN THE KITCHEN!
MAYBE IT DIDN'T SEE--?
WHUFF FFFF!
EXIT
RrrRRR?

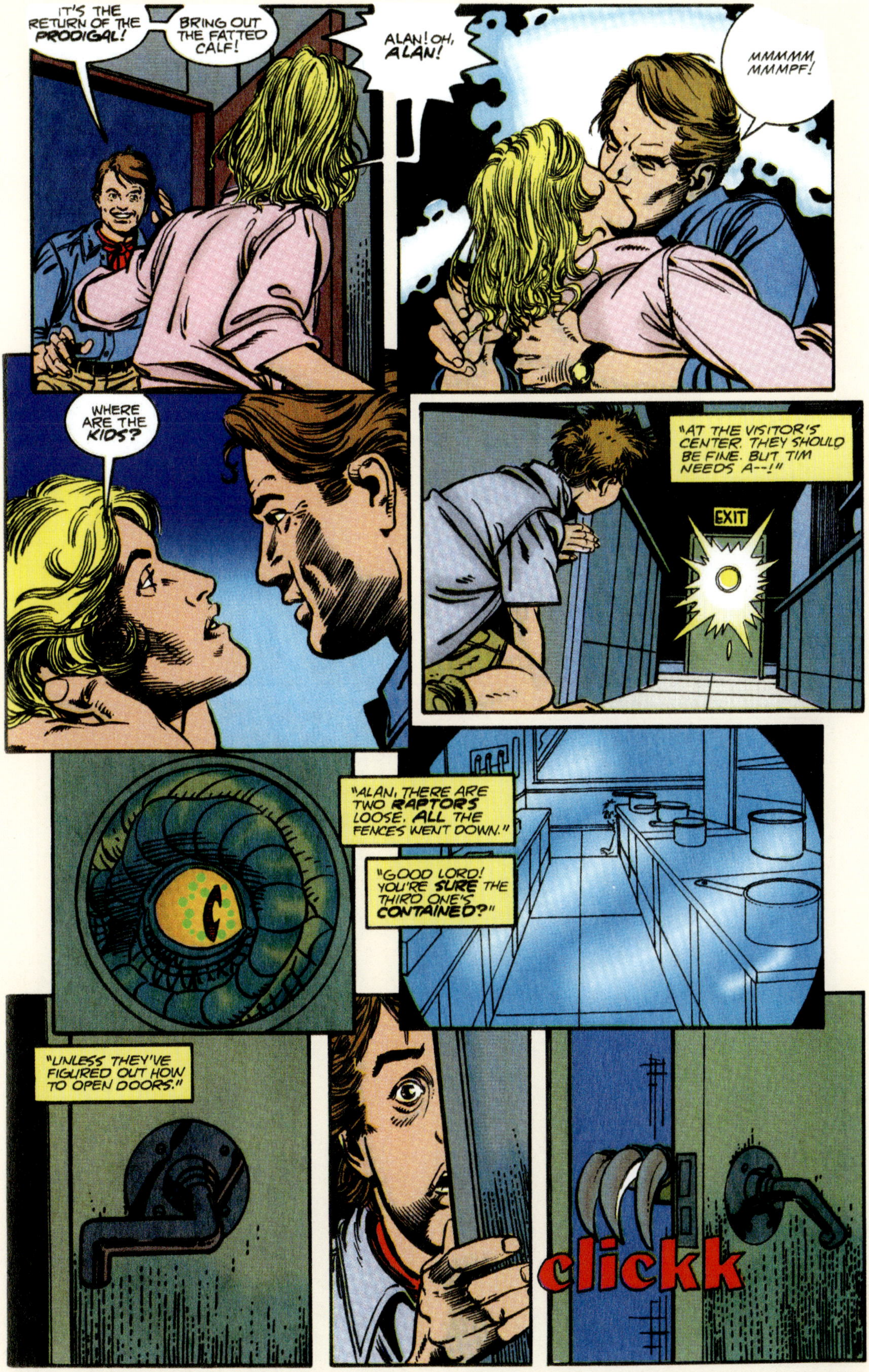

IT'S THE RETURN OF THE PRODIGAL!
BRING OUT THE FATTED CALF!
ALAN! OH, ALAN!
MMMMM MMMPF!
WHERE ARE THE KIDS?
"AT THE VISITOR'S CENTER. THEY SHOULD BE FINE. BUT TIM NEEDS A--!"
EXIT
"ALAN, THERE ARE TWO RAPTORS LOOSE. ALL THE FENCES WENT DOWN."
"GOOD LORD! YOU'RE SURE THE THIRD ONE'S CONTAINED?"
"UNLESS THEY'VE FIGURED OUT HOW TO OPEN DOORS."
clickk

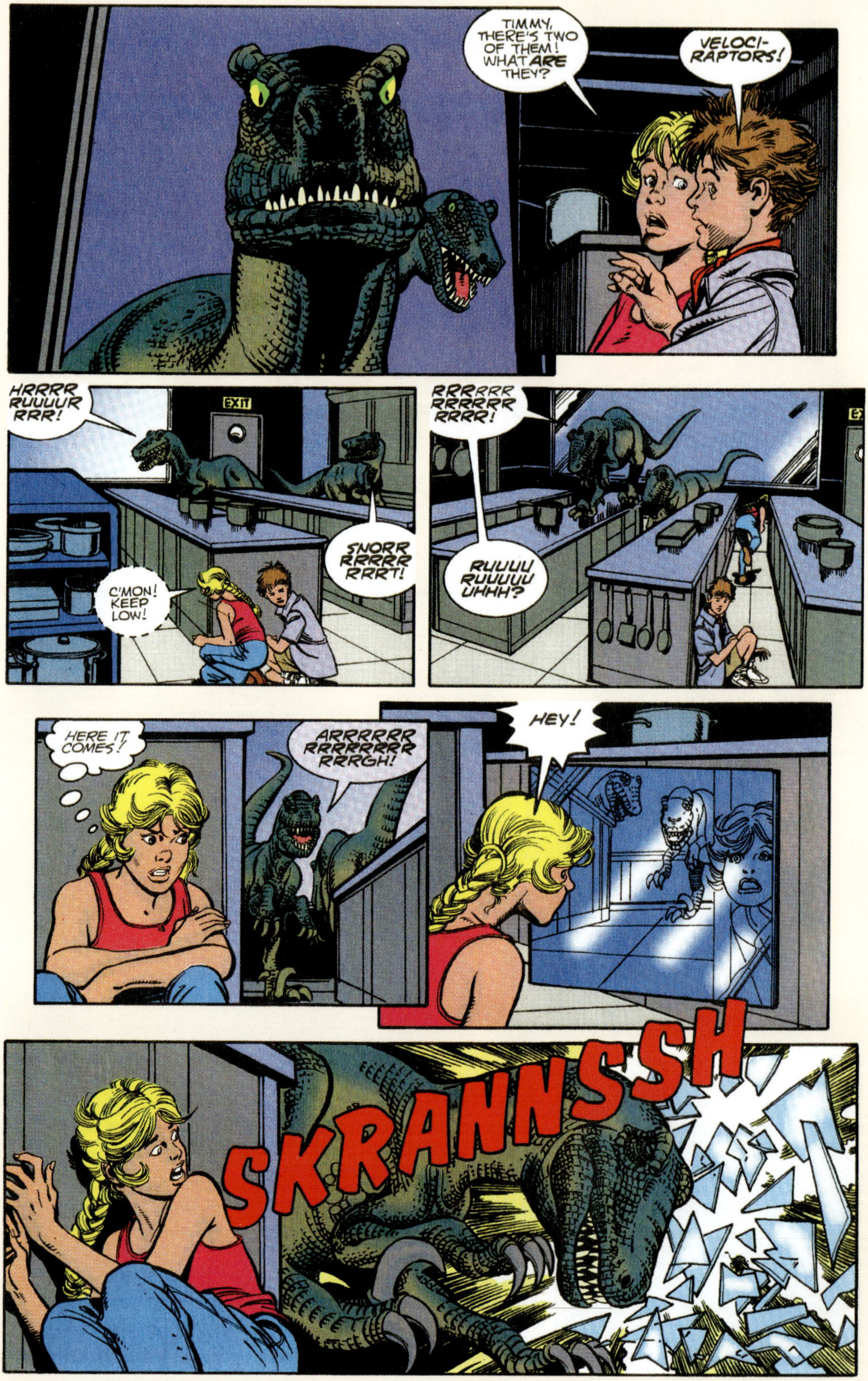
TIMMY, THERE'S TWO OF THEM! WHAT ARE THEY?
VELOCI-RAPTORS!
HRRRR RUUUUR RRR!
EXIT
SNORR RRRRR RRRT!
C'MON! KEEP LOW!
RRRRRR RRRRRR RRRR!
RUUUU RUUUUU UHHH?
HERE IT COMES!
ARRRRRR RRRRRRR RRRGH!
HEY!
SKRANNSSH

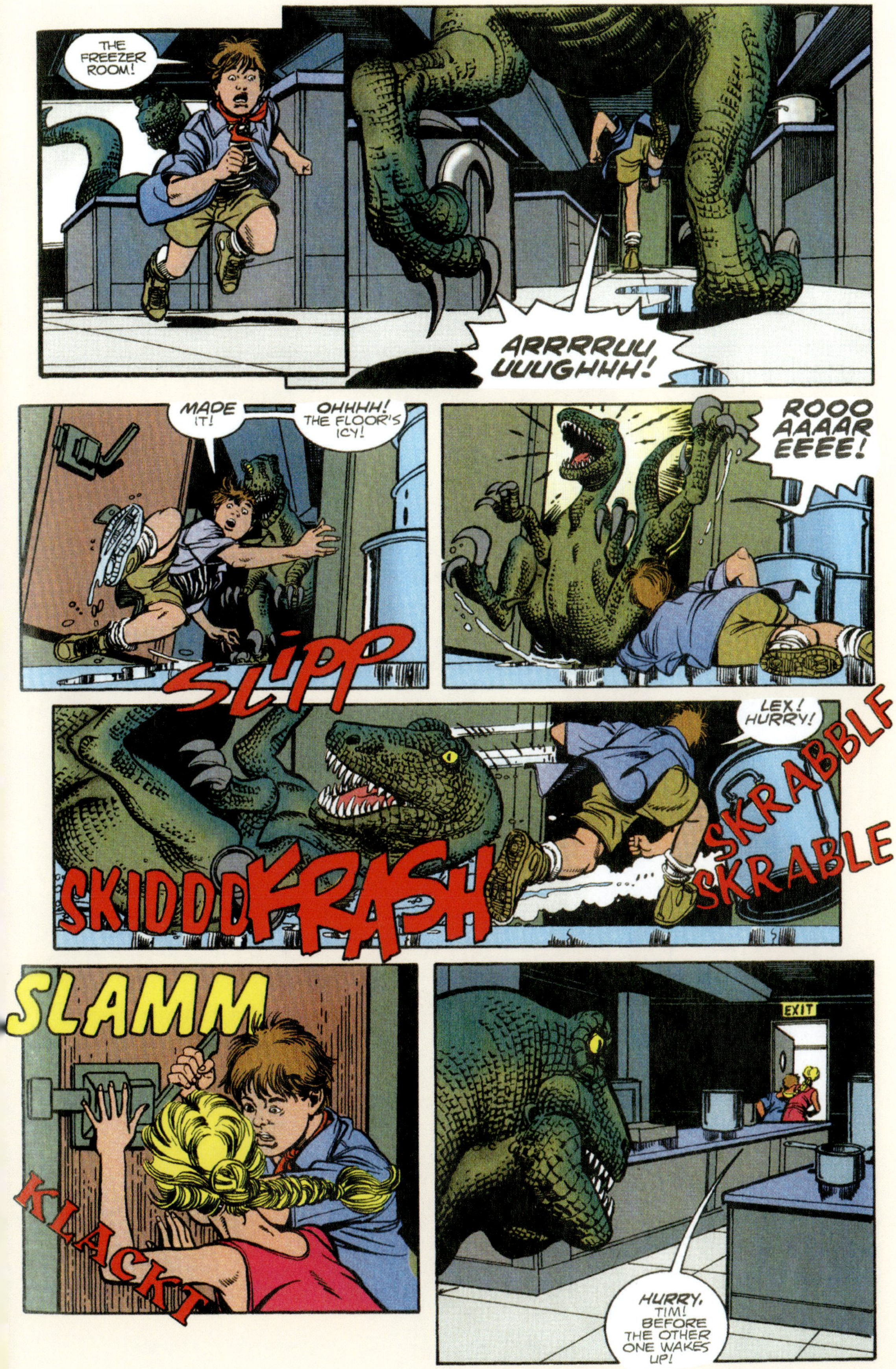
THE FREEZER ROOM!
ARRRRUU UUUGHHH!
MADE IT!
OHHHH! THE FLOOR'S ICY!
SLIPP
ROOO AAAAR EEEE!
LEX! HURRY!
SKIDDD KRASH
SKRABBLF SKRABLE
SLAMM
KLACKT
EXIT
HURRY, TIM! BEFORE THE OTHER ONE WAKES UP!

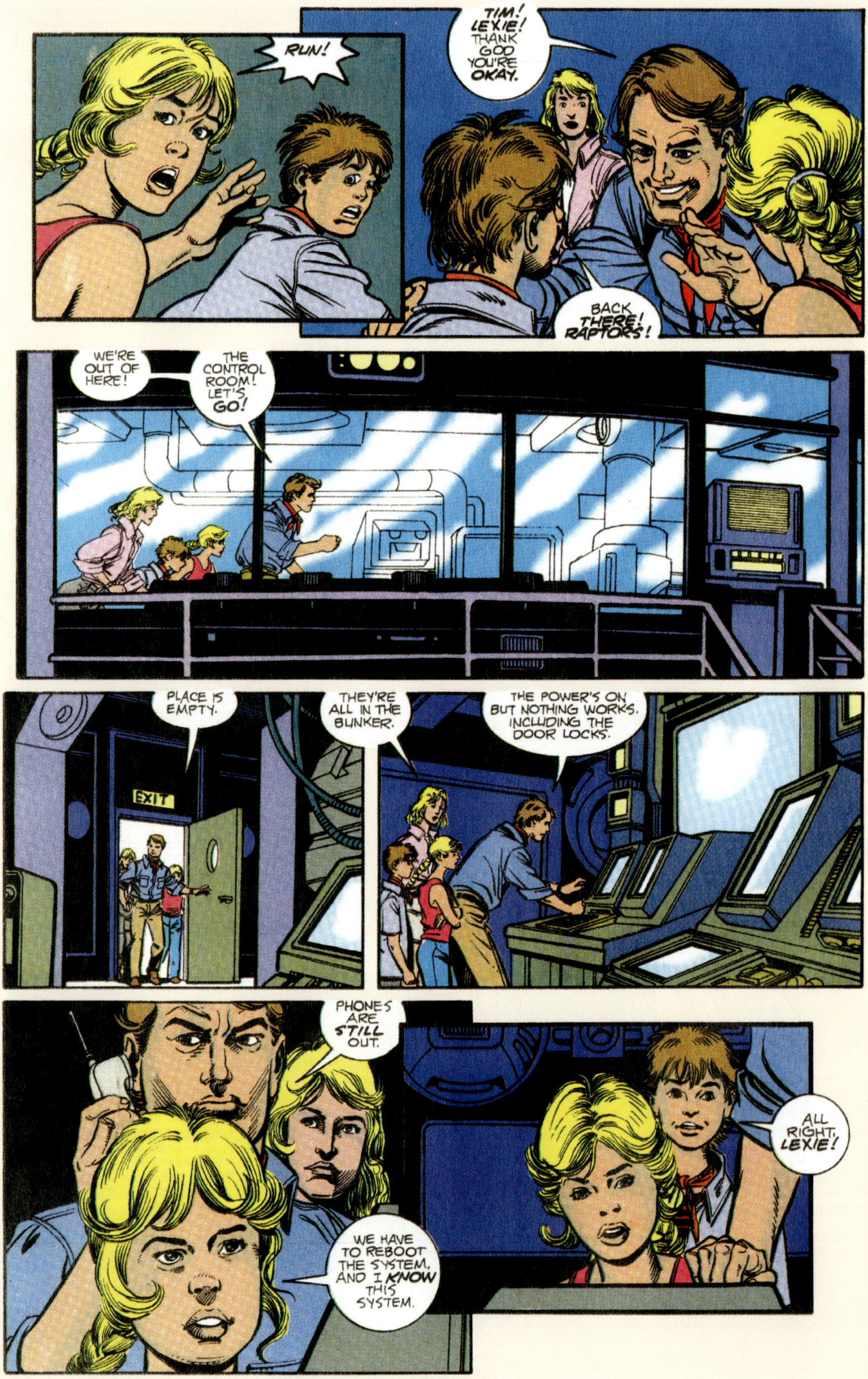
RUN!
TIM! LEXIE! THANK GOD YOU'RE OKAY.
BACK THERE! RAPTORS!
WE'RE OUT OF HERE!
THE CONTROL ROOM! LET'S GO!
EXIT
PLACE IS EMPTY.
THEY'RE ALL IN THE BUNKER.
THE POWER'S ON BUT NOTHING WORKS. INCLUDING THE DOOR LOCKS.
PHONES ARE STILL OUT.
WE HAVE TO REBOOT THE SYSTEM. AND I KNOW THIS SYSTEM.
ALL RIGHT, LEXIE!

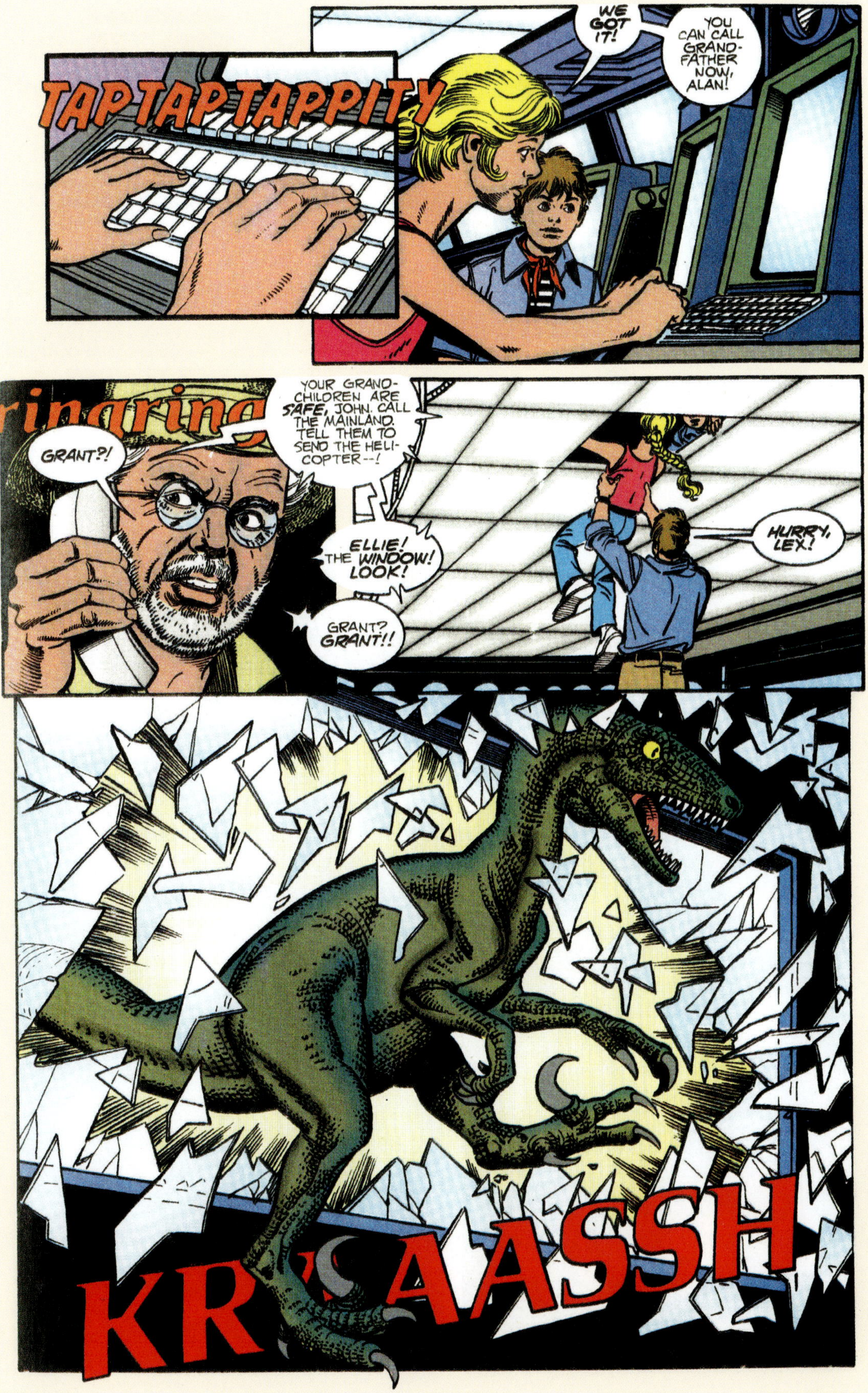
TAPTAPTAPPITY
WE GOT IT!
YOU CAN CALL GRAND-FATHER NOW, ALAN!
ringring
GRANT?!
YOUR GRAND-CHILDREN ARE SAFE, JOHN. CALL THE MAINLAND. TELL THEM TO SEND THE HELI-COPTER--!
ELLIE! THE WINDOW! LOOK!
GRANT? GRANT!!
HURRY, LEX!
KRAASSH

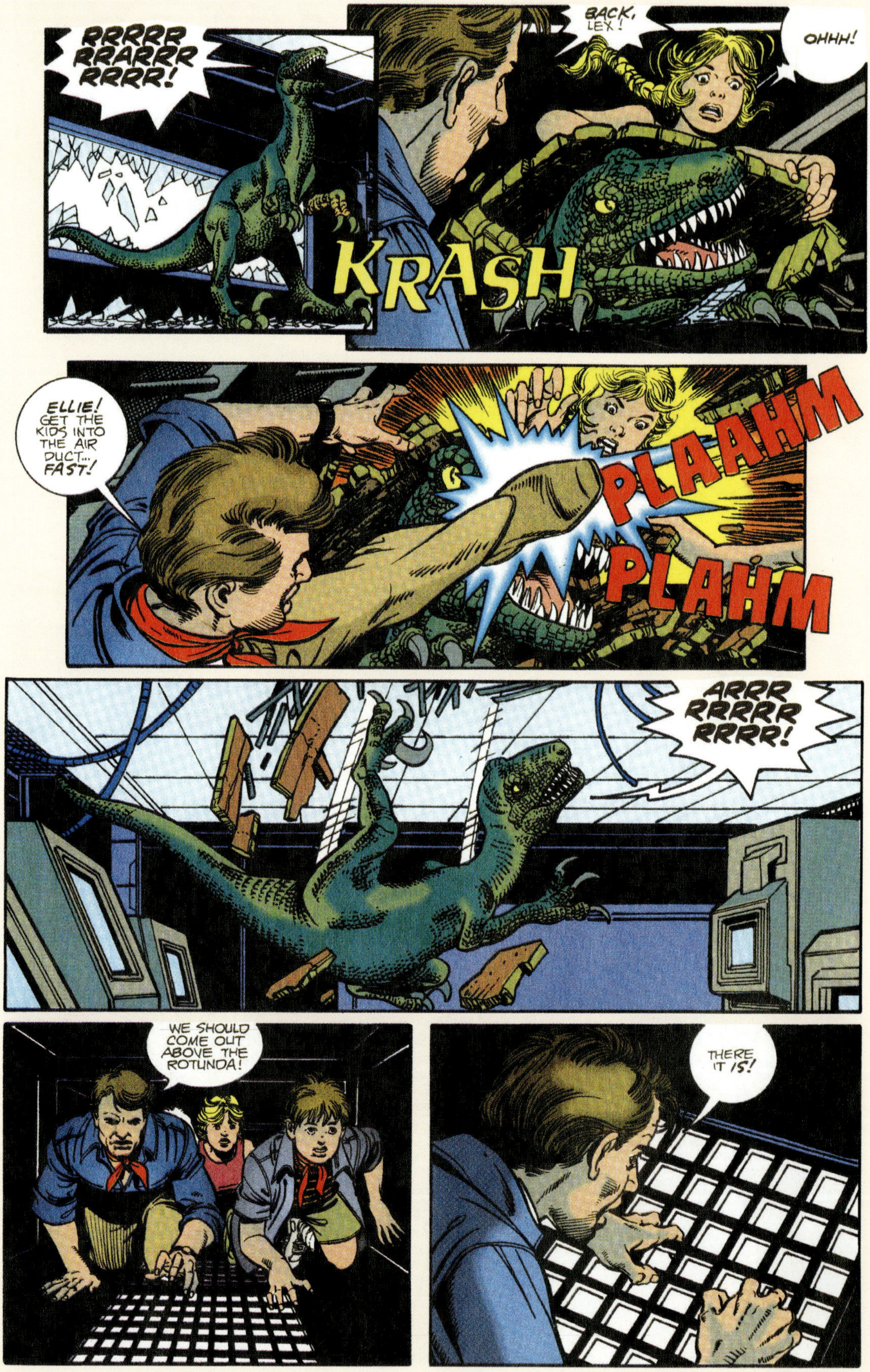
RRRRR RRARRR RRRR!
BACK, LEX!
OHHH!
KRASH
ELLIE! GET THE KIDS INTO THE AIR DUCT... FAST!
PLAAHM
PLAHM
ARRR RRRRR RRRR!
WE SHOULD COME OUT ABOVE THE ROTUNDA!
THERE IT IS!

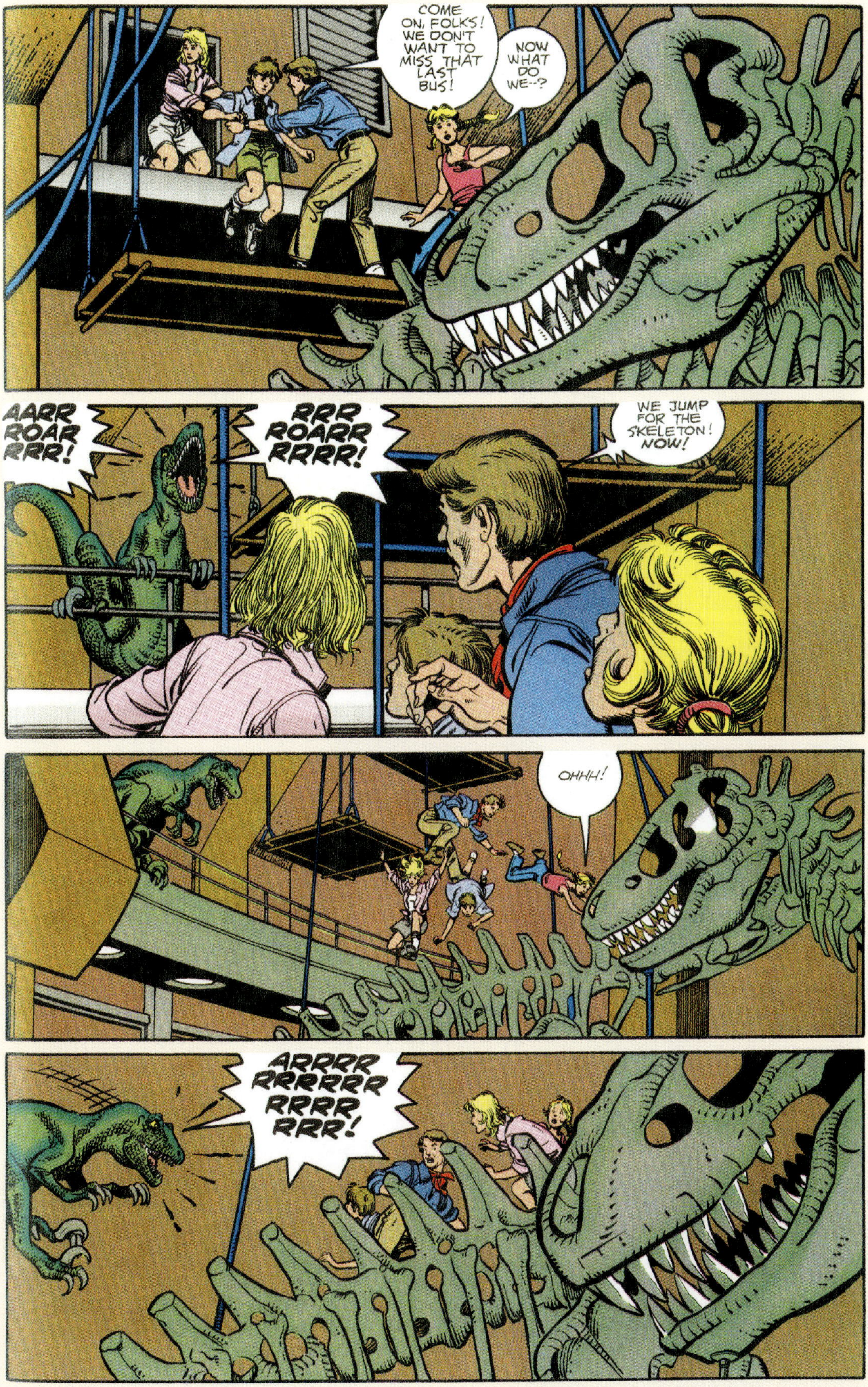
COME ON, FOLKS! WE DON'T WANT TO MISS THAT LAST BUS!
NOW WHAT DO WE--?
AARR ROAR RRR!
RRR ROARR RRRR!
WE JUMP FOR THE SKELETON! NOW!
OHHH!
ARRRR RRRRRR RRRR RRR!

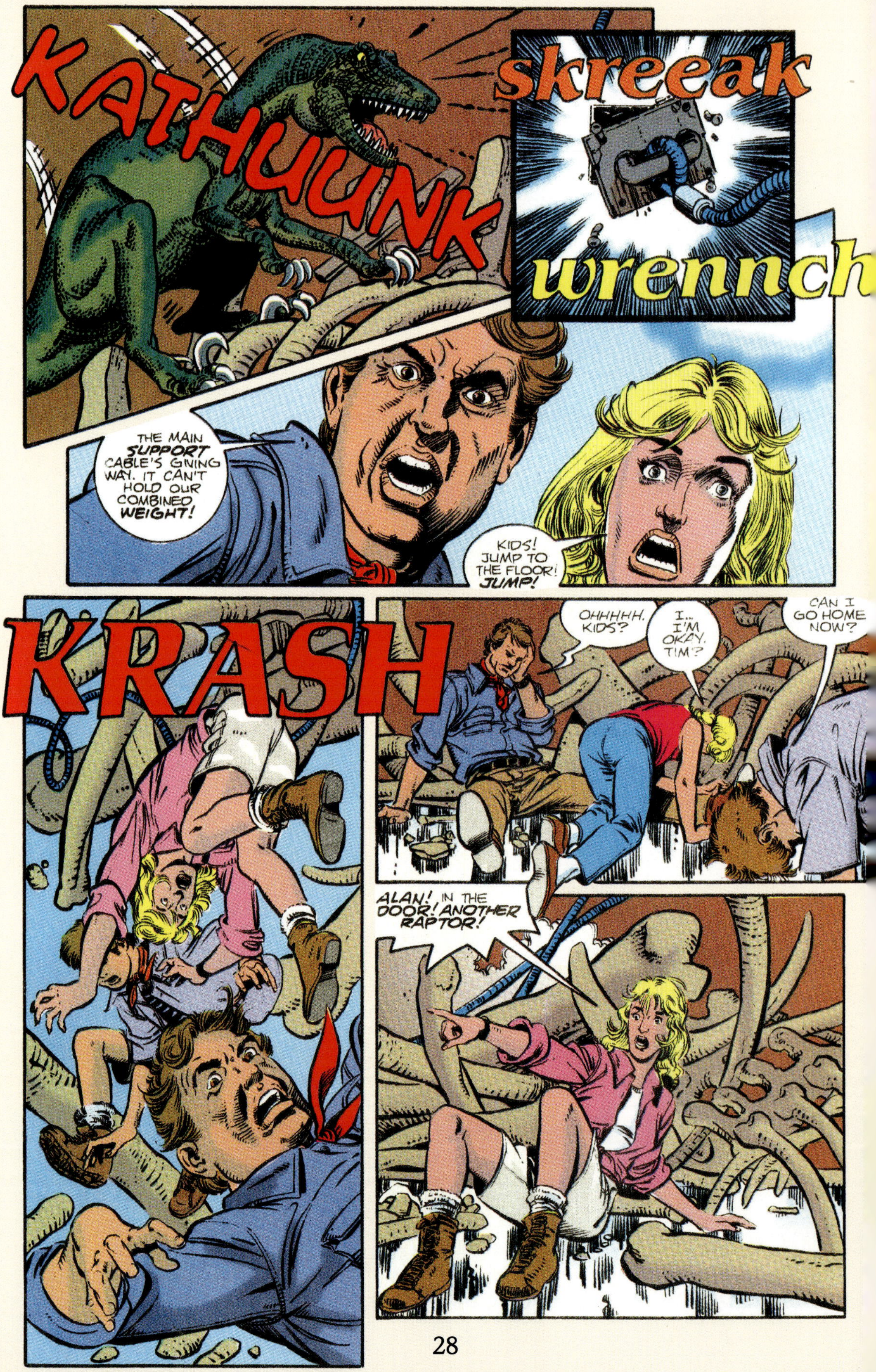
KATHUUNK
skreeak
wrennch
THE MAIN SUPPORT CABLE'S GIVING WAY. IT CAN'T HOLD OUR COMBINED WEIGHT!
KIDS! JUMP TO THE FLOOR! JUMP!
KRASH
OHHHHH. KIDS?
I... I'M OKAY. TIM?
CAN I GO HOME NOW?
ALAN! IN THE DOOR! ANOTHER RAPTOR!

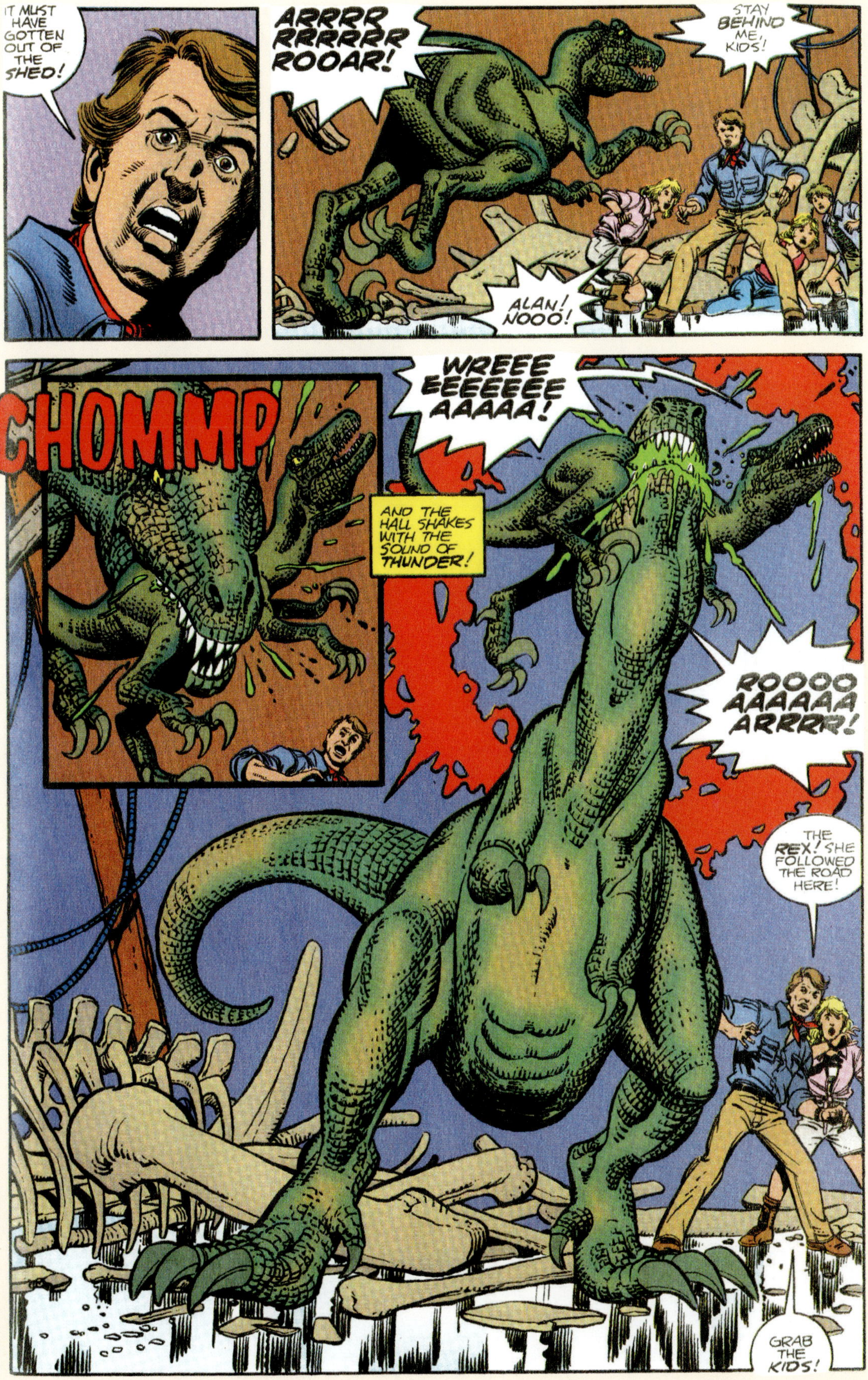
IT MUST HAVE GOTTEN OUT OF THE SHED!
ARRRR RRRRRR ROOAR!
STAY BEHIND ME, KIDS!
ALAN! NOOO!
CHOMMP
WREEE EEEEEEE AAAAA!
AND THE HALL SHAKES WITH THE SOUND OF THUNDER!
ROOOO AAAAAA ARRRR!
THE REX! SHE FOLLOWED THE ROAD HERE!
GRAB THE KIDS!

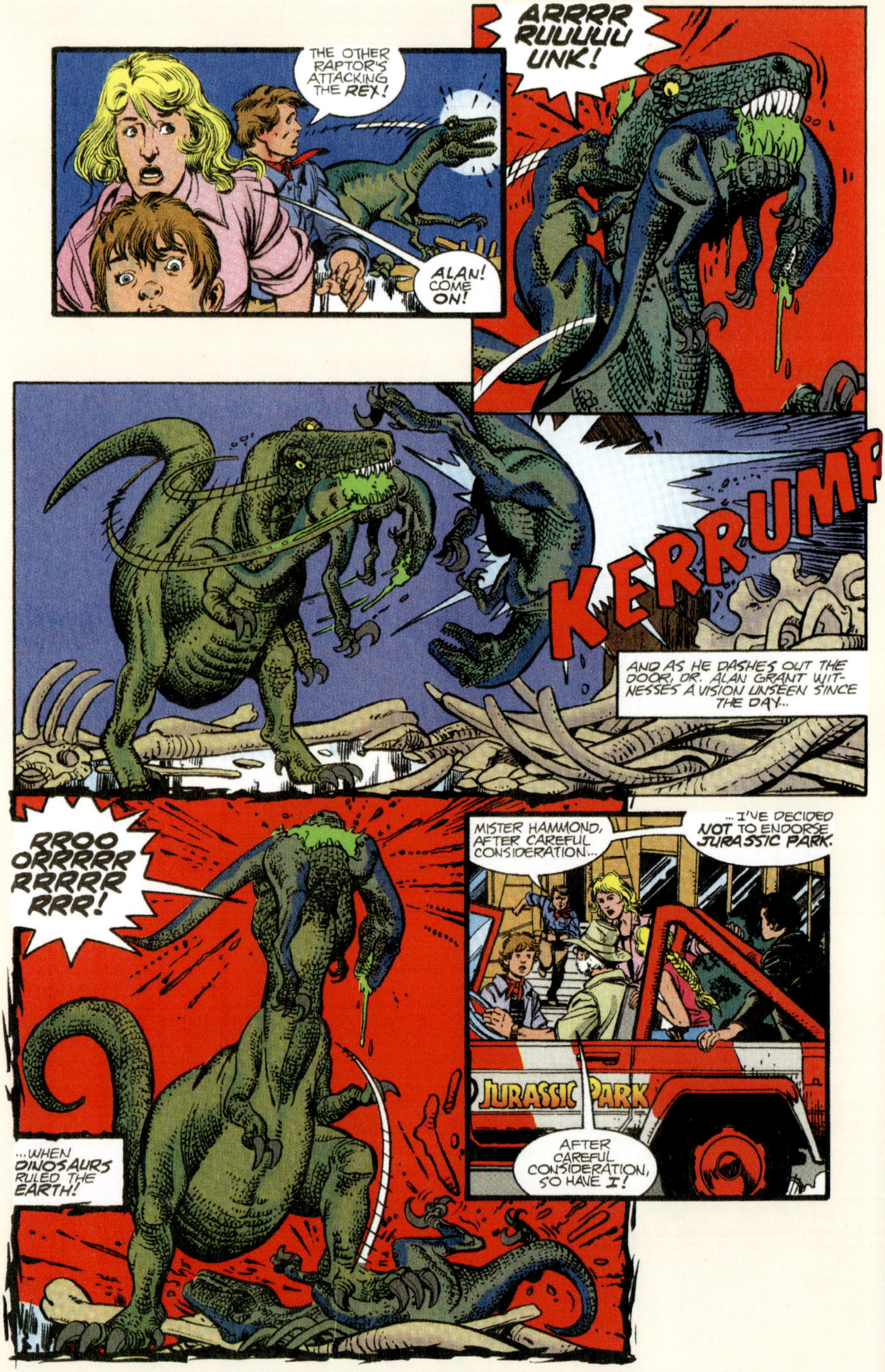
THE OTHER RAPTOR'S ATTACKING THE REX!
ALAN! COME ON!
ARRRR RUUUUU UNK!
KERRUMP
AND AS HE DASHES OUT THE DOOR, DR. ALAN GRANT WITNESSES A VISION UNSEEN SINCE THE DAY...
RROO ORRRRR RRRRR RRR!
...WHEN DINOSAURS RULED THE EARTH!
MISTER HAMMOND, AFTER CAREFUL CONSIDERATION...
...I'VE DECIDED NOT TO ENDORSE JURASSIC PARK.
JURASSIC PARK
AFTER CAREFUL CONSIDERATION, SO HAVE I!

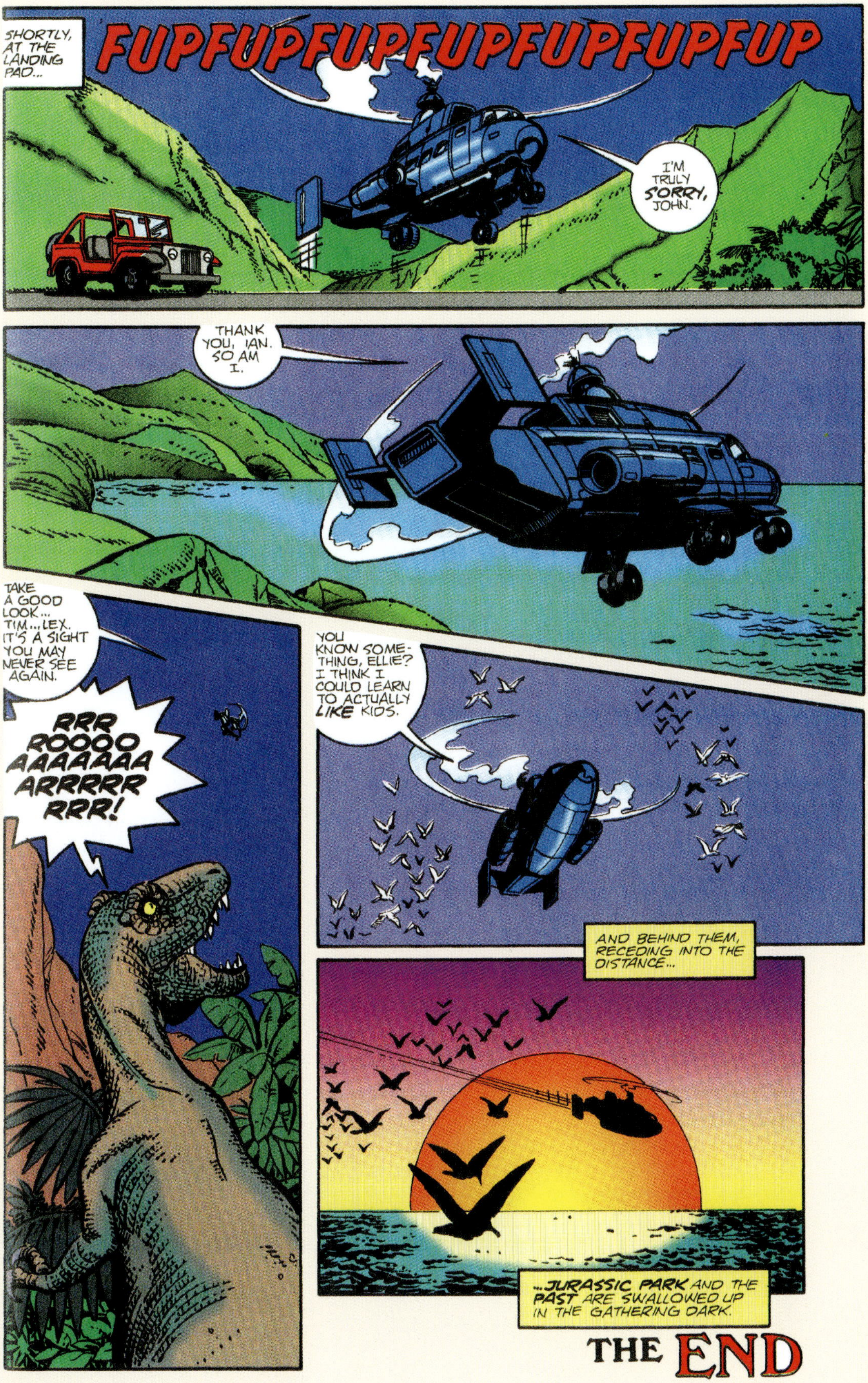
SHORTLY, AT THE LANDING PAD...
FUPFUPFUPFUPFUPFUPFUPFUP
I'M TRULY SORRY, JOHN.
THANK YOU, IAN. SO AM I.
TAKE A GOOD LOOK... TIM... LEX. IT'S A SIGHT YOU MAY NEVER SEE AGAIN.
RRR ROOOO AAAAAAA ARRRRR RRR!
YOU KNOW SOME-THING, ELLIE? I THINK I COULD LEARN TO ACTUALLY LIKE KIDS.
AND BEHIND THEM, RECEDING INTO THE DISTANCE...
...JURASSIC PARK AND THE PAST ARE SWALLOWED UP IN THE GATHERING DARK.
THE END